SPECIAL MESSAGE TO READERS

THE ULVERSCROFT FOUNDATION
(registered UK charity number 264873)

was established in 1972 to provide funds for research, diagnosis and treatment of eye diseases. Examples of major projects funded by the Ulverscroft Foundation are:-

- The Children's Eye Unit at Moorfields Eye Hospital, London
- The Ulverscroft Children's Eye Unit at Great Ormond Street Hospital for Sick Children
- Funding research into eye diseases and treatment at the Department of Ophthalmology, University of Leicester
- The Ulverscroft Vision Research Group, Institute of Child Health
- Twin operating theatres at the Western Ophthalmic Hospital, London
- The Chair of Ophthalmology at the Royal Australian College of Ophthalmologists

You can help further the work of the Foundation by making a donation or leaving a legacy. Every contribution is gratefully received. If you would like to help support the Foundation or require further information, please contact:

THE ULVERSCROFT FOUNDATION
The Green, Bradgate Road, Anstey
Leicester LE7 7FU, England
Tel: (0116) 236 4325

website: www.foundation.ulverscroft.com

THE BLACK HUNCHBACK

After researching the legend of the treasure of Langley Towers, Sir Owen Langley informs his daughter Pauline that he has discovered the hidden meaning of the doggerel verse left behind by an ancestor as a clue to its hiding place. But then he mysteriously disappears, after rushing out of the house in the middle of the night in his pyjamas! On the same night, the legendary figure of the Black Hunchback — the sinister family spectre that haunts the Towers and heralds death — is spotted by Pauline on the lawn . . .

GERALD VERNER

THE BLACK HUNCHBACK

Complete and Unabridged

LINFORD
Leicester

First published in Great Britain

First Linford Edition
published 2017

*A catalogue record for this book is available
from the British Library.*

ISBN 978–1–4448–3169–6

Published by
F. A. Thorpe (Publishing)
Anstey, Leicestershire

Set by Words & Graphics Ltd.
Anstey, Leicestershire
Printed and bound in Great Britain by
T. J. International Ltd., Padstow, Cornwall

This book is printed on acid-free paper

1

The Shadow on the Lawn

Pauline Langley woke with a start, her nerves quivering with an undefinable sense of fear!

For some seconds, she lay staring with wide-open eyes at the hazy whiteness of the ceiling, in that intermediate state between full consciousness and dreamy unreality which usually follows the sudden awakening from deep sleep.

The curtains of her bedroom window were not drawn, and a bright shaft of silvery moonlight streamed into the room, its rays lying half across the foot of her bed and ending in a vivid splash of light upon the lemon-coloured walls beyond.

For some time she remained motionless, trying vainly to recall what it was that had so suddenly interrupted her sleep. At last, she raised herself upon one elbow and felt about on the little table beside her bed for her watch. Glancing at the dial in the dim reflected glow from the ray of moonlight, she saw that it was just two o'clock; and, even as she looked, from somewhere in the house came the soft tones of a bell as a clock chimed the hour.

A slight shiver ran through her as she laid the little wristwatch back on the table, an unaccountable feeling of dread that seemed to steal like an icy liquid through her veins. And yet the night was warm enough — hot, in fact, one of those sultry oppressive nights in midsummer when the silence is so intense that it can almost be felt.

She was wide awake now; all vestige of sleep had disappeared; and, pushing back the bedclothes, she slipped out and drawing a soft silken scrap about her bare shoulders, searched about on the floor for her slippers. Having found them and put them on, she sat for a second or two on the edge of the bed, listening.

Not a sound reached her ears. The night was absolutely still and quiet. What was it, then, that had so suddenly wakened her? Surely nothing tangible. But, even as the thought passed through her mind, again there stole over her that vague feeling of inexplicable dread — of approaching evil.

With a little exclamation of annoyance that she should have allowed her imagination to play tricks with her, and convinced that further sleep, for the time, at least, was impossible, she again searched the little table and found her cigarette case and matches. Lighting a cigarette, she rose and crossed to the window.

The scene that met her gaze as she looked out was one of almost fairy-like beauty.

Langley Towers was a long, low, rambling building of lichen-covered grey stone, built in the shape of a T. At each end of the shorter arm rose the squat square towers that gave the house its name.

Pauline's bedroom window overlooked a wide expanse of velvety lawn, bounded on one side by a high yew hedge, and on the other by a dense shrubbery of rhododendron bushes. At the end of the lawn, stone steps led downwards to the Rose

Garden, now a mass of flaming colour, the perfume of which reached the girl's nostrils through the open window; and beyond, past the orchard, rose the curve of the heavily wooded hills with which the house was surrounded on three sides.

Almost as clear as if seen in the light of day, save that it was curiously softened — and, it seemed, endowed with a touch of enchantment — the picture bathed in the light of the full moon unrolled itself to the girl's eyes.

The long, greyish-purple shadows from the tall pine trees behind the rhododendrons fell athwart the smooth, pearly-green of the lawn, motionless and still. The sky was cloudless, and not a breath of wind stirred so much as a leaf. It seemed as if the very spirit of peace had taken up its abode in the place, and was hovering brooding over the whole. And yet in spite of the almost perfect beauty of the night and the atmosphere of restfulness and tranquillity, the girl still felt that extraordinary feeling of unexplainable fear!

Suddenly she drew in her breath with a

sharp hiss, and the cigarette fell from her fingers and lay, unheeded, smouldering on the carpet. Away at the end of the lawn by the shrubbery, something had moved! A vaguely darker shadow within the shadows of the pines seemed to have shifted further out over the grass!

Unconsciously, Pauline Langley's hands clenched until the nails bit into the soft flesh of her palms, as she strained her eyes to make out its shape. But everything was motionless again. Nothing stirred.

Had it been only her imagination — a trick of the moonlight? She bent down and picked up the smouldering end of the cigarette from where it had burned a black charred mark on the carpet. Even as she straightened up again, she saw that it was not her imagination.

A shadow was moving slowly across the moonlit expanse of turf — an indefinite, shapeless shadow, without outline or meaning!

Almost holding her breath in her fear, the girl watched, fascinated. Gliding stealthily from one shadow thrown by the pines to another, the darker shadow advanced towards the house. It was every minute growing more and more distinct — was taking definite shape and forming before her eyes.

She longed to scream, to run, to tear herself away from the window, but something had made her throat dry and husky, and shod her feet with leaden weights. She was rooted to where she stood, helpless, unable to speak or move, unable to do anything but stare unceasingly at that ominous, silent, uncanny shadow on the lawn.

The story of the old legend of Langley Towers ran through her mind. The Black Hunchback! The shapeless figure in black that was supposed to haunt the Towers! The shadow was drawing nearer, nearer, and now it had taken definite form . . . a squat, ugly dwarfed shape . . . grotesquely resembling a human body . . .

Suddenly, from somewhere in the house a door banged noisily, followed by the sound of running footsteps!

The noise broke the spell over the girl, and with a hoarse, scarcely audible cry, she ran to the door and tore it open. The corridor outside was pitch dark, for it turned sharply at right angles, and so the window at the further end failed to give any light to the other part.

As she felt along the wall for the electric switch, the girl heard another door shut with a bang. It seemed to come from somewhere in the lower regions. Finding the switch, she pressed it down and felt somehow relieved as the passage became flooded with light. Before advancing further, she stood listening; but after that last noise of the shutting door all was still and silent again as the grave.

Pauline Langley was not a girl who usually suffered from that extremely modern ailment which seems to be the excuse for a multitude of sins, and comes under the general heading of *nerves*! On the contrary, she was a healthy girl who spent much of her time in the open air, which possibly accounted for her wonderful natural complexion that owed nothing of its beauty to artifice, but was purely a product of fresh air and sunshine.

And yet, at that moment, she was seized with a violent fit of trembling and dizziness, and had to cling for a moment to the wall for support. The sense of terror which had been ever present since her awakening had grown stronger.

With a supreme effort of will she pulled herself together, and started to walk down the corridor in the direction of the staircase. She had made up her mind to seek her father.

The banging doors apparently had not disturbed the sleeping household, for everything remained quiet. Sir Owen Langley's bedroom was on the next floor, and, as quickly as her still trembling limbs would let her, the girl made her way to the end of the passage and down the stairs to the floor below.

Her father's room was at the end of the corridor, and like her own, faced the back of the house overlooking the lawn. As she neared the door she suddenly stopped, her heart beating wildly. For it was wide open!

Presently she advanced a step further and entered the room. It was flooded with moonlight that streamed in through the window, the curtains of which had apparently been harshly torn aside, for one of them was partly ripped from the rings which supported it. But the room was empty!

The bedclothes had been hurriedly pushed back, and her father's dressing gown, which usually hung over the foot of the bed, was missing. He had evidently gone out in a hurry. But why? While she was pondering thus, there suddenly came from outside in the grounds a sharp cry, followed almost instantly by the sound of two shots in quick succession!

With a feeling as if an icy hand had suddenly closed round her heart, Pauline flew to the window. Between the shadow of two of the pine trees which sprawled across the lawn, clearly visible in the moonlight, lay the figure of a man, and the girl felt herself go suddenly cold as she saw that it was wrapped in the peculiar mauve colour of her father's silk dressing gown! And then she saw something else — a vague shadow which seemed to hover, vulture-like for a second close to the body on the ground. A shadow shapeless and undefinable, but curiously sinister . . .

For a moment the girl swayed clutching at the curtains, and then with a cry she slipped to the floor in a dead faint!

2

The Legend

Anthony Vyne, star reporter on *The Daily Messenger*, sat hunched up in the carved oak chair before his littered writing-table. His fingers tapped ceaselessly on the arms, while his right foot beat an impatient tattoo on the floor. Anthony was feeling perturbed. For nearly a week *The Daily Messenger* had been without news of importance, and Sims, the News Editor, was becoming impossible. Prominence had been given to the paper's scheme of insurance and such items of interest as were available, had been written up to their fullest extent. But nothing that it was possible to twist into a front-page splash had broken. True, all the other dailies were in the same predicament, but that did not console Anthony Vyne in the least, and he felt that it was time he pulled off some stunt that would justify his existence in the eyes of the powers that be.

'Get *The Messenger*, and see what Vyne has to say about it,' had become a slogan, as well-known as 'Keep that schoolgirl complexion!' It was heard as often in Brixton as in Bond Street; indeed, there was no class of man or woman in London who did not know and appreciate the work of Anthony Vyne.

Nothing annoyed Anthony more than the manufacturing of 'stunt news,' and he had spent the best part of the previous night wandering aimlessly round London in the hope of finding a 'story' but without avail. Tired out, and thoroughly fed-up, he had at last sought his flat and bed only to find that, owing to the sultriness of the night and the restlessness of his brain, he was unable to sleep. At half-past six he gave up the attempt and rising, bathed and dressed and sought his study.

The room in which Anthony did most of his work was a key to the man's character. The furniture, the rugs, the rare etchings, all betokened a man of taste, and their arrangement portrayed the artist. It was possibly this very artistic strain that had made him the success he undoubtedly was, for he possessed the ability to see something in the world's events that men of coarser sensibilities missed, and the aspect that he saw was always more interesting than other people's, and to this he owed his position in the Street of Ink.

At Scotland Yard he was considered an asset by the police, for on many occasions his peculiar sensitiveness had discovered features in a case that had been overlooked even by highly trained detectives, and so charming was his manner that he never made enemies, owing, no doubt, to the fact that in addition to this charm of manner, he was in the habit of allowing the kudos to rest with the police, contenting himself with the knowledge that he had got a story for *The Messenger* and beaten his rivals.

Presently, with an impatient exclamation, Anthony suddenly pulled the telephone towards him with the intention of ringing up his friend, Jack Darrell, and inviting him round to breakfast.

A greater contrast could not be imagined than Anthony Vyne and his friend, Darrell, and many people wondered at the friendship, but few knew of the bond that held them together.

They had been at school together, indeed, Darrell had been Anthony's fag, and Vyne had been instrumental in saving Darrell's life at the risk of his own during a bathing episode. This incident had made Anthony Darrell's hero, and being blessed with a good portion of the world's wealth, he had constituted himself, after leaving school, a sort of general factotum to Anthony, and accompanied him on most of his adventures. Just as Anthony was tall, dark, and aristocratic in appearance, so was Darrell short, fat and plebeian, and it was rumoured that certain facetious gentlemen of Fleet Street had dubbed them Mutt and Jeff, but this was no doubt due to the jealousy that is said to exist between brothers of the pen.

Certain it was that these two understood each other, and it is possible that the very contrast of Darrell's slow, almost stolid, brain, was a help to the quick, penetrating, almost intuitive mind of Anthony Vyne.

Anthony was just about to lift the receiver when his man entered carrying a card in his hand.

'I wasn't certain that you were up, sir,' he said. 'But there's a young lady downstairs who wishes to see you urgently — very urgently, she said.'

Anthony took the card from him and glanced at it in surprise.

'Ask Miss Langley to come in,' he said, pushing the telephone away from him and rising to his feet. Frost withdrew, and the reporter remained for some seconds twisting the thin piece of pasteboard about in his fingers. He had met Pauline Langley several times with her father, whom he knew well. What could be the reason of the girl's early call? It must be something very urgent to have brought her all the way from Buckinghamshire at such an hour.

A tap at the door put an end to Anthony's musings, and Frost stood aside as Pauline entered the room.

A tall, fair girl, dressed plainly in a well-cut costume of blue serge, the little fashionable closely fitting hat she wore set off the perfect oval of her face with its deep limpid blue eyes, small uptilted little nose, and perfectly shaped mouth.

Anthony noticed as he stepped forward to greet her that there were dark shadows beneath her eyes, and that the lids were slightly swollen as though she had been recently crying.

'Good morning, Miss Langley,' said Anthony as he wheeled forward a chair. 'I am awfully glad to see you again, though I cannot imagine to what I am indebted for the pleasure of this visit.'

The girl sank into the deep comfortable armchair with a sigh of relief, and started nervously to remove one of her gloves.

It was some seconds before she spoke, and during the short silence which intervened, Anthony Vyne's grey eyes rapidly took in every detail of her appearance. Evidently she had quite recently recovered from some violent shock to her nerves for her hands, as they fumbled with the buttons of her gloves, were trembling violently, although she was doing her utmost to master her emotions.

'I hope, Mr. Vyne,' she said at last, in a musical voice, 'that you will forgive me for troubling you at such an early hour. But knowing that you were a friend of father's, I thought that — that — ' She broke off nervously.

'There's no need to apologise,' said the reporter with a smile. 'I shall be only too pleased if I can help you in any way. Tell me at once what it is that is troubling you.'

'It is very nice of you,' she replied gratefully, the ghost of a smile breaking at the corners of her pretty mouth and lighting up the shadows of her face. 'I was sure that you would help me — daddy has often spoken about you, and so, of course, I determined to come to you before going to the police — Oh, Mr. Vyne, I'm so worried, I'm sure that something dreadful has happened to daddy!' She stopped short, her voice breaking into a little sob.

'Come, come, Miss Langley,' said Anthony

gently. 'Your nerves are in pieces. You must try and pull yourself together. I suppose you have come straight up from Buckinghamshire?'

'I thought of you immediately,' she answered in a voice that shook, in spite of her efforts to keep it steady, 'and left at once.'

'And I suppose you didn't have time for any breakfast,' Anthony continued. 'Now you really must — '

'Oh no, really,' she protested; 'I couldn't eat anything.'

'Well, in any case, you'd better have some coffee,' answered the reporter, as he crossed the room and rang the bell. 'It'll do you good, and then you can tell me what it is that's worrying you.'

The steaming coffee which Frost presently brought, had the effect of soothing the girl's shattered nerves, and after she had set her cup down, Vyne perched himself on the edge of the table, and thrust his hands deep into his trousers pockets.

'Now, Miss Langley,' he prompted, 'tell me all about it.'

'I hardly know how to begin,' she

commenced nervously, after a little pause. 'It was about two o'clock this morning that I suddenly awoke from a deep sleep. What it was that caused me to waken I don't know, but I was conscious of being filled with a horrible sense of fear.

'Finding after a time that it was impossible to go to sleep again, I rose and lit a cigarette, hoping that the smoke would make me feel drowsy. It was a beautiful night — bright moonlight, but hot and oppressive — and I went over to the window and looked out.

'My room overlooks the lawn, and in the light of the moon everything was almost as clear as day. Suddenly, as I stood at the window, my strange unaccountable sense of fear increased. It may seem silly and childish to you, Mr. Vyne, but it is impossible to explain the awful terror I felt at that moment.

'There were many shadows on the lawn, and all at once I was certain that one of these, a squat shapeless shadow, had moved and was coming nearer towards the house. The story of the legend which runs through our family came to my mind — the figure known as the Black Hunchback, which is supposed to warn a Langley of approaching death.

'Just then I heard the sound of a door bang in the house below, and the noise of running feet. It seemed to come from daddy's room, but I couldn't be sure. However, mastering my overwhelming sense of fear, I left my room and descended the stairs to his bedroom which is on the floor below and directly under mine. Another door banged as I reached the corridor.

'When I got to father's room I found the door wide open, and the room empty. His window also overlooks the lawn, and as I crossed the threshold I heard a cry from outside, followed by two shots! I rushed at once to the window, and saw the body of my father lying on the grass and bending over him a squat dwarfish form — the figure of the Black Hunchback of the legend!'

She paused to regain her breath. She had told the story so vividly that Anthony Vyne felt a sudden quickening of his pulses, and a slight thrill urge through his veins. A gleam of interest crept into his eyes, but he made no remark, waiting for the girl to finish her story.

'I think I must have fainted after that,' she continued presently, 'for the next thing I remember was finding Hume, our butler, bending over me.

'When I had fully recovered my senses, he told me that he had been awakened by the sounds of the shots, and had come down to see what was the matter. On passing daddy's door, he had been surprised to find it open, but merely thought that daddy, too, had been awakened by the noise. Looking in, however, he saw me lying in front of the window, and finding that I had fainted, had stayed with me until I had come round.

'I told him at once what I had seen. By this time the whole household was aroused, and Hume, leaving me in the care of Mrs. Wakefield, the housekeeper, went out into the grounds, to see what had happened to father. In a short time he returned. I think he thought I had been dreaming, for he said that there was not a sign of anything on the lawn, and everything was silent. Of daddy there was not a trace.

'At first, of course, I was greatly relieved, and I began to think that perhaps, after all, the whole thing was only due to my imagination. As the time passed, however, and still there was no sign of daddy, I began to get worried.

'Hume awakened Yates, the chauffeur, and accompanied by the gardener, they made a close search of the grounds, calling daddy's name repeatedly. I had completely recovered from my fainting fit by now and, with Mrs. Wakefield, went out on to the lawn to the spot where I had, or thought I had seen daddy lying.'

A little shudder passed over her at the recollection, but she continued almost immediately.

'Mr. Vyne, it had not been my imagination. On the grass, which was vet with dew, was the distinct impression left by something heavy which had rested there, and by the side of this were several drops of fresh blood!

'You cannot imagine the horror I felt at this discovery. I was convinced that some dreadful fate had overtaken daddy, and then I remembered you and instructed Yates to get the car out. It was then about five o'clock, and daddy had been missing for nearly two and a half, hours. Mr. Vyne, do you think you could come to Langley Towers, and find out what has happened to daddy? I know of no one else to whom I can go, and I'm so dreadfully worried.'

'I must get on to my paper and obtain permission first,' answered Anthony. 'But I don't think there will be any difficulty. It's an extraordinary story, Miss Langley, and I'm intensely interested.'

'Then you will come,' cried the girl, her eyes shining. 'You can't think how grateful I am.'

'It's I who should be grateful,' smiled Anthony.

He hurried to the telephone. 'Excuse me a moment,' he said, and picked up the receiver. A few seconds later the melancholy voice of Sims floated over the wire. Anthony told him briefly the girl's story.

'It might lead to just the scoop we're looking for,' he concluded.

Sims grunted.

'I don't suppose there is anything in it,' he said pessimistically, 'but still, it will give you a good excuse for loafing about the country for a few days. Try it, anyway, and God help you if you haven't a front page story by tomorrow night!'

There was a click as he hung up the receiver, and Anthony hurried again to the girl.

'That's all right,' he said cheerfully; 'now I should like to ask you a question or two.' He rose to his feet, and selecting a cigarette from the box on his writing-table, obtained Pauline's permission and lighted it. Returning to the table he resumed his previous position. For several seconds he remained silent, while the curling blue smoke from his cigarette wreathed round his head and floated ceilingwards.

'Of course, there is always the possibility,' he remarked at length, 'which we mustn't ignore, that Sir Owen is absenting himself for some very good reason of his own.'

'But daddy was only wearing his pyjamas and dressing gown,' protested the girl. 'He could not go very far dressed like that, and if he had still been in the grounds he would have answered when Hume and Yates called to him.'

'Yes, I suppose he would,' agreed the reporter. 'I only suggested it as a possibility. It's scarcely a probability, however. When you looked out of the window on hearing the shots what made you come to the conclusion that the figure lying on the lawn was that of Sir Owen?'

'I recognised daddy's dressing gown,' answered Pauline. 'It is of a peculiar mauve colour — quite unmistakable.'

'You didn't actually see his face, then?' queried Anthony.

The girl shook her head.

'No,' she replied; 'I only saw his dressing gown. But it is unlikely that anyone else would be wearing it except daddy.'

Anthony drew in the smoke of his cigarette and inhaled deeply before speaking, then he asked:

'The sound of the two shots — did they seem near or far away?'

'Oh, quite near; just outside the window.'

'And was there any appreciable lapse of time between the first shot and the second?'

'No,' she answered; 'in fact, they seemed almost together.'

'Of course, you can think of no reason to account for Sir Owen's strange disappearance,' said Anthony. 'For instance, he hadn't, so far as you know, any enemies who would be likely to try and cause him harm?'

'Not to my knowledge,' she declared. 'Daddy was very popular with the people in the neighbourhood. In fact, everyone who knew him liked him. He was not a man who made many friends — not intimate friends, I mean — but this was because he spent most of his time in the library and seldom went out anywhere. You see, he believed he had discovered a clue to the Langley Treasure!'

Anthony Vyne looked up quickly at the girl's last remark, his eyes alight with interest.

'The Langley Treasure,' he repeated. 'What is that?'

'It is connected with the story of the

Black Hunchback,' she replied; 'in fact, I believe that it was the origin of the legend of the ghost that is supposed to haunt our family. I never believed in it much, but daddy always seemed to take it seriously.'

'I should rather like to hear the story,' said Anthony.

'But surely, Mr. Vyne,' Pauline protested, 'an old legend which happened hundreds of years ago can have nothing to do with daddy!'

'Directly — no; but indirectly — yes,' answered Vyne. 'And it is a rule of mine never to let slip a scrap of information that is likely to have any bearing, however vague, on the matter on which I am engaged. In this instance, it appears to me to have a direct bearing, as you yourself stated a few seconds ago that Sir Owen took it quite seriously and was very much interested in it.'

'If you think it is important,' said Pauline, 'I'll try and tell you the story, though I'm afraid I don't know very much about, it, except what I have heard now and again from daddy.'

Before she could say any more,

however, a tap at the door interrupted her.

'Come in,' said Anthony, with a frown, which cleared as soon as he saw who the visitor was.

'Hello, Jack!' he exclaimed. 'You're early.'

Jack Darrell's fat face wreathed in a smile.

'I thought if you had the day free, we might take a run in the car down to — ' He broke off, as he caught sight of the girl, and would have backed out with a muttered apology if Anthony hadn't stopped him.

'It's all right, Jack,' said the reporter, introducing them, and briefly recounted for his friend's benefit the reason for Pauline's early visit.

Darrell listened intently, his small twinkling eyes alight with interest. Vyne turned to the girl after he had finished.

'I am sorry to have interrupted you,' he apologised, 'but I want Darrell to have a clear idea of the whole affair from the beginning, because if I am to help you I shall find his services very necessary. If you will now continue, I assure you that I am all attention.'

'As far as I can remember,' began Pauline, 'the legend of Langley Towers dates back to about the year one thousand, one hundred and ninety three. Part of it at least is a matter of history, and deals with the capture of Richard Coeur de Lyon, by Leopold Duke of Austria. You'll probably know more about that than I. Richard, on leaving Palestine, was blown from his course, and his ship wrecked on the Adriatic coast. While trying to cross Germany, he was captured by Leopold, who eventually had to surrender his prisoner to Henry Sixth, then Emperor of Germany, who demanded a ransom for the safe return of Richard to England.

'King John, who was at that time ruling over England in the absence of his elder brother, saw in this a chance to prevent Richard returning and depriving him of the throne. While openly pretending to be doing all in his power to raise the necessary ransom, he was in reality doing his utmost to keep Richard a prisoner in Germany.

'Now, as far as I can remember, the legend goes that Robin Hood, the outlaw of Sherwood Forest — from which, by the way, our family first took its name — was a close friend of Richard's, and as soon as he heard that Richard had been made prisoner by Henry, he decided to find the money needed for his ransom. He knew that it was impossible for himself to convey the money to London, as there was a price on his head, so he arranged with his friend, Sir Ralph Lang-Lee — who was an ancestor of ours and a loyal supporter of Richard — to receive the money, which was in the form of bullion, at his house, Lee Towers in Buckinghamshire, and from thence convey it to London in his own name.

'The spies in the employ of King John soon got to hear of this arrangement, and one of them, a dwarf by the name of Shard, by some means or other managed to become one of the party who were in charge of the bullion, and who were to convey it from Sherwood to Lee Towers. King John's plan was to have the bullion intercepted during this part of the journey, but at the last minute Robin Hood changed the date and despatched it a day earlier than was originally intended. This threw all John's carefully laid plans out of action. The bullion arrived safely at Lee Towers, and Sir Ralph made preparations to convey it in person to London on the following day. Then on the night before they were to leave for London, Sir Ralph suddenly became aware that the house was surrounded by spies in the employ of King John.

'The story runs that fearing lest an attack should be made on the Towers, and the bullion fall into the wrong hands, Sir Ralph, unknown to anyone in the house, hid the chest which contained it, and cancelled his proposed journey. The dwarf, Shard, who had arranged for the bullion to be seized on its way from Lee Towers to London, tried to communicate the altered plans to his accomplices outside, and was caught in the act by Sir Ralph. In his anger at the discovery, Sir Ralph strangled him, but the exertion caused him to break a blood-vessel.

'Knowing that he was dying, and

getting weaker every moment from loss of blood, he called for parchment and ink and wrote down a clue to the hiding place of the bullion chest, which he directed was to be put in the hands of Robin Hood. Eight hours later he died.

'Almost immediately after his death, an attack was made upon Lee Towers, during which the paper containing the clue to the hidden chest was lost. I believe it is supposed to have been hidden by one of Sir Ralph's servants, who was afraid it would fall into the hands of King John's spies. Anyhow, it was found later and is now in father's library. The name Lang-Lee became contracted years after to that of Langley, and my father's great-great-grandfather, Sir Maurice Langley, changed the name of the house to Langley Towers.

'The ghost of the Hunchback Shard in his black jerkin and doublet, is supposed to haunt the Towers, appearing as a warning of death or disaster to the members of our family, becoming known as the Black Hunchback. I'm afraid I've told the story very badly, Mr. Vyne, but there is an old manuscript in daddy's library that sets the whole thing down in detail.'

As she came to the end of her story, Anthony rose to his feet, and threw the stub of his cigarette into the fireplace.

'It's a most interesting story, Miss Langley,' he remarked, selecting another and lighting it. 'The treasure was never found, of course?'

The girl smiled, and shook her dainty head.

'No,' she replied, 'although several members of our family have searched for it for years without result. As I have said, daddy was very interested, and latterly believed that he had hit upon a clue.'

'What is the clue supposed to have been written by Sir Ralph before he died and now in your father's library?' asked Darrell.

'No one could ever make head or tail of it,' replied Pauline. 'It's just a short verse of nonsense. If there is any truth in the story of the treasure, I think Sir Ralph must have been delirious when he wrote it.'

Anthony laughed. Whatever Sir Owen might think about the legend of Langley Towers, it was clear that his daughter regarded the whole story as pure imagination.

'I suppose you can't remember the verse?' he enquired.

'Oh, yes,' she answered; 'I've heard it so often that I know it by heart. It runs like this:

' 'The arrow from the bow, released
In one direction only goes
Be it North, South, West or East.
But not from where the wind blows
Where at length it comes to rest,
Seek there and ye shall find in chest.'

'Isn't it dreadful nonsense?'

'It certainly doesn't sound very illuminating,' replied the reporter, frowning. 'But at the same time there may be some hidden meaning to it that no one has yet discovered. I should like to have a look at the original and also the detailed account of the legend.' He paused for a moment, staring with unseeing eyes at a blue smoke ring that was gently floating upwards from his cigarette.

'When you looked out of your father's window,' he continued presently, 'and saw what you thought was his body lying on the lawn, you mentioned that you also saw something that appeared to be bending over him. What was this something?'

Pauline's face went pale, and when she spoke her voice sounded curiously husky.

'It was horrible, a shapeless, vulture-like, shadowy thing. I only saw it for a moment, but it seemed to be — ' She paused. ' — the figure of a hunchback!'

'You are certain you didn't imagine it?' asked Anthony. 'Don't think me rude — but under the circumstances, don't you think it might have been caused by a shadow — some curiously shaped branch or foliage?'

'I'm certain it was real,' said the girl decidedly. 'What it was I don't know, but I'm prepared to swear that it was something tangible.'

Anthony Vyne sat motionless for some minutes, then he turned abruptly to Darrell.

'You might ask Frost to let us have

breakfast at once, old chap,' he said. 'And ask him to pack a couple of suitcases also. We shall be returning with Miss Langley at once.'

Darrell jumped up with alacrity. The strange story had fired his imagination, and he was anxious to get to the scene of action. As he reached the door, Anthony stopped him.

'And you might also tell Frost to give Miss Langley's chauffeur some breakfast, too,' he added.

The stout man nodded, and he had barely left the room when the telephone bell rang sharply. Anthony stepped quickly to the instrument and unhooked the receiver. After a moment's conversation, he turned to Pauline.

'It's for you,' he said, 'from Langley Towers.'

The girl sprang to her feet and took the receiver from Anthony's outstretched hand.

'Perhaps they have had news of daddy,' she cried hopefully. She had scarcely been at the 'phone a moment before she uttered a sharp cry, and the receiver dropped from her fingers and swung at the end of its cord. Vyne leaped forward in alarm at sight of her white set face.

'What has happened?' he asked quickly.

'Oh!' she gasped, as she clung to the reporter's arm for support. 'I have just had a message from Hume. Something evil is at large round Langley Towers. They have just discovered the dead body of Travis, the head gamekeeper, in the Home Covert, shot through the heart!'

3

The Strange Behaviour of Mr. Frank Cunningham

It was a little over two hours later that the big Daimler car containing Anthony Vyne, Jack Darrell, and the girl, turned into the chestnut-bordered drive that led up to the main entrance to Langley Towers. It had been a pleasant run in the beautiful warm summer sunshine, and the big car had made good going, reeling the miles swiftly behind them with the regularity of clockwork.

By the time they arrived, they were all beginning to feel decidedly hungry, for Darrell and Vyne had made but a hasty breakfast, and the girl had refused to eat anything at all until Anthony had insisted, and then he could only persuade her to nibble at a small piece of dry toast.

The sunlight filtering through the interlaced branches of the magnificent chestnuts spread an ever-changing dancing carpet of gold in the path of the car as it rolled swiftly up the well-kept drive. Presently they rounded a bend and caught their first glimpse of the house.

At one time a moat had surrounded Langley Towers, but this had long since dried up and had been filled in so that only a slight rise in the ground proclaimed where it had once been. With the filling in of the moat had also occurred the removal of the drawbridge, and its place had been taken by a flight of lichen-stained stone steps. The original massive iron-bound oaken door, however, remained, and above it the space where once the portcullis had hung. Anthony Vyne, who loved picturesque old architecture, eyed the ivy-covered rambling mansion with approval. As the car drew to a halt at the foot of the steps, the heavy front door swung open, and an elderly white-haired man came down to greet them, followed by a footman who took charge of the suitcases.

'There is still no news of daddy, Hume, I suppose?' asked the girl as she descended from the car, and was helped out by Darrell.

The white-haired old butler shook his head sadly.

'No, Miss,' he replied, 'not a sign. The master seems to have vanished into thin air, and on the top of that there's the death of Travis. Terrible doings — terrible doings! The police have arrived already — Inspector Person is in the Home Covert now.'

'How did they get to hear of it so soon?' enquired Anthony.

'I telephoned, sir, immediately on the discovery of the body,' answered Hume, with dignity. 'I understand that it was the proper procedure.'

'Oh, yes, you did quite right,' said the reporter. 'I was hoping,' he added to Darrell, 'that we should have had time for a look round before the police arrived. Miss Langley, I should like first of all to see the Home Covert where the body of the gamekeeper was found. Perhaps Hume could show us the way.'

'It's all right, Hume,' Pauline said; 'Mr. Vyne is a friend of my father's, and he and Mr. Darrell have kindly come down to try and help me find out what has happened to him.'

The butler bowed, and in a few minutes they were following the stately figure of the old man across the lawn in the direction of the sunk rose garden and the wooded hillside beyond.

A high crumbling grey stone wall separated the rose garden from the rest of the estate, and about half way along this was a stout door of oak. It stood half open, and passing through the three walked quickly along a narrow footpath which wound in and out among the trees, and presently came in sight of two uniformed figures who appeared to be searching among the bushes which thickly covered the ground in this vicinity. They straightened up at the sound of the approach of Anthony, Darrell and the butler, and proved to be an Inspector of police, and a constable.

Inspector Person was a short, fat man of decidedly bucolic appearance, with a rather large flowing moustache of a bright and vivid red hue, which together with a pair of pale watery blue eyes that protruded from his head in an alarming manner, gave him somewhat the appearance of a cross between a genial codfish and a walrus.

Anthony introduced himself, and the Inspector regarded him with great interest as he heard the name which *The Messenger* had made famous throughout England.

'Mr. Vyne,' he said in a deep voice, 'I'm h'afraid that this is 'ardly in your line. My opinion is as 'ow it's just an ordinary poaching affair.'

'Possibly you're right, Inspector,' replied Anthony pleasantly. 'However, as I happen to be on the spot I'm sure you'll have no objection to my just having a look round.'

'With pleasure,' said Inspector Person. 'This is the body. Poor Travis — a nice chap 'e was — one of the best.' He led the way over to a small clump of bushes by the side of which lay the body of a tall, bearded man. One arm was flung rigidly out at right angles to the body, the fingers clenched. The other arm lay straight down by the side. A deep stain of blood spread over the velvet waistcoat in the region of the heart.

Anthony Vyne stood for some seconds gazing down at the face, and then he simply dropped on to one knee beside the body, concentrating his attention on the clenched hand. Then he drew from his pocket his powerful lens and closely examined the stained waistcoat. After a few moments he looked up.

'There are distinct signs of scorching,' he remarked, looking up at Person. 'The shot must have been fired at close range. It came from a revolver or an automatic, I should say.'

The Inspector nodded his large head in agreement.

'The doctor said the same thing,' he replied ponderously. 'He said that death must 'ave been h'instantaneous.'

'It hardly fits in with your theory of poachers though, does it?' said Anthony, and turned his attention again to the closed hand. 'Poachers rarely carry revolvers or automatics with them.' While he was talking he had been gently forcing back the curved fingers, and now he straightened up holding in his hand a small object that glittered in the straggling rays of sunlight that penetrated the foliage above them.

Darrell bent eagerly forward. 'What is it?' he asked, excitedly.

Anthony Vyne held it out in the palm of his hand, and the Inspector and his friend looked at it with interest.

It was a small golden ball of the kind that is often worn upon the end of a watch chain, and which opens out into the form of a cross, the interior being covered with masonic symbols. From the tiny ring at its apex, two or three links of fine gold chain still remained. Clearly, it had been torn from the end of some chain or other.

'I don't know 'ow I came to miss that,' declared Inspector Person, his voice full of chagrin; 'I never thought of lookin' in 'is 'and.'

Anthony smiled as he rose to his feet, and brushed his trousers. There was a thoughtful expression on his round good-natured face, and Darrell could see that somehow or other his friend had read in the finding of the golden charm a great deal more than any of the rest — himself included.

'H'it rather h'upsets my idea of the poachers, don't it?' continued Person. 'What is your opinion, Mr. Vyne?'

'I'm afraid, Inspector,' answered Anthony, 'that it's too early in the affair for me to advance any opinion yet. I am positive of one thing, however, that it is not the work of poachers. Who was the first to find this poor fellow?'

'The gardener, sir,' broke in Hume. 'Would you like to speak to him? He's in the rose garden.'

'Presently,' said Anthony; 'I haven't quite finished here yet.' He commenced to examine the ground at close proximity to the body. It had been fairly well trampled by the large boots of Inspector Person and the constable, and after a few minutes Vyne saw that it was hopeless to seek for any traces among that heterogeneous collection of footprints. He returned to the remains of the gamekeeper, and stooping down closely inspected the soles of his boots. A strange little gleam lit up his pale eyes as he turned to Hume a moment later.

'Now,' he said, 'I should like to see the gardener if you'll take me to him. I expect I shall see you later, Inspector. In any case, I will let you know at once if I find anything fresh.'

Inspector Person looked disappointed at not being asked to accompany the reporter, but he made no audible comment.

On their way back towards the house Anthony seemed in a rather thoughtful mood. Once, however, he spoke to Hume.

'You didn't say anything to the police about the disappearance of Sir Owen?' he asked.

The butler shook his grey head.

'No, sir,' he replied. 'Miss Langley told me not to mention it to anyone until after she had seen you, and I instructed the servants likewise.'

Vyne nodded his approval.

'I think it just as well not to mention it at the moment,' he agreed.

They had reached the rose garden by now, and very soon espied the figure of the gardener at work in one corner. Hume left them here and returned to the house. Old Edwards, the gardener, proved to be a garrulous old fellow, not at all averse to a little gossip.

Anthony Vyne was a past master in the art of securing information from a witness, and in a few minutes he and the old man were on the friendliest of footings. It appeared that Edwards had discovered the body of Travis quite by accident, having gone into the Covert to secure sticks for tying up some flowers, about half-past seven.

'And h'it's a very peculiar thing, sir,' he remarked, 'a very peculiar thing. I went past the place much earlier this morning, and could 'ave sworn it weren't there then, and I've been within earshot of the place h'ever since, and never heard no sound.'

Anthony shot a quick side glance at Darrell, a glance which considerably puzzled his friend, for there was a gleam of triumph in it the meaning of which Darrell could not account for.

'You can't fire guns with h'out making a noise,' continued the old man, 'leastways 'uman beings can't.' His voice dropped to a whisper as he uttered the last words.

'You surely don't imagine Travis was killed by a ghost?' asked Anthony smiling.

Old Edwards looked at him with a peculiar expression.

'Aye, you can laugh, sir,' he said seriously, 'but there be strange 'appenings round 'ere lately. Mebbe you've heard tell of the legend of the Towers. They say in the village that the Black Hunchback 'as appeared again. I ain't seen it — I 'ope to 'Eaven I never may, for it means death to those what claps eyes on it — but I know one what did see it — ' He broke off.

'And is the person still alive?' enquired Vyne smiling. The old man shook his head.

'No,' he replied slowly. ''E's dead right enough — it were Travis!'

Jack Darrell felt a cold sensation in the region of his spine, in spite of the almost tropical heat of the day, at the gardener's quietly spoken words.

'So Travis saw the Black Hunchback,' said Anthony thoughtfully; 'when was this?'

‘It were about three days ago,’ replied old Edwards, looking pleased that his words had created such an impression. ‘’E told me all about it the next morning when we met for our usual pint together at the Prodigal’s Return in the village. ’E were out on duty as usual, and about three ’o’clock, just as it were beginning to get light, ’e thought ’e ’eard somebody moving about among the trees in the ’Ome Covert.

‘At first ’e thought it was a poacher, and crept up near to where ’e ’ad ’eard the sound, but by the time ’e got there all was quiet. ’E listened but ’e couldn’t ’ear another sound, and began to think that ’e ’ad been mistaken. All at once ’e saw among a bit of shrubbery something movin’. ’E ’ollers to it, but as ’e didn’t get no reply, ’e starts to chase it. ’E says the thing, whatever it was, was goin’ in the direction of the Towers. ’E could ’ear it moving about through the trees, but ’e couldn’t see much of it being a cloudy night and raining — presently ’e came to a small clearing in the wood, and there ’e saw it real plain. ’E says it was the figure of a twisted 'unchback, dressed in something black and without no face to it. 'E was that scared 'e didn't go no further, and the thing vanished. I reckon it was the Black 'Unchback all right, seeing as what 'as happened to Travis poor chap,' concluded the gardener.

'Did he mention what he had seen to anyone else but you?' asked Anthony, who seemed keenly interested in the old man's story.

'Oh, aye,' replied Edwards, nodding his head. ''E told Sir H'Owen the next morning. But Sir H'Owen told 'im not to be silly and not to say nothing about it, as 'e didn't want those sort of rumours gettin' about. It's my belief Sir H'Owen would 'ave done well to 'eed what poor Travis was telling 'im.'

'Do you think that Sir Owen's disappearance has got anything to do with this Black Hunchback bogey?' Anthony enquired.

The gardener paused for some seconds before he replied.

'So you knows about Sir H'Owen's disappearance, eh?' he said at last. 'Well, we was told not to mention it, but seein' as 'ow you knows all about it, what I'm goin' to say can't do no harm.' He stopped and took a quick look all round him as if to make certain that no one was listening before he proceeded.

'As I said before, sir, there be strange 'appenings round 'ere lately. There's somethin' evil at work round the Towers, and it don't bode no good for anyone of the name of Langley. I'm only an old man, sir, and maybe you and the young gentleman are laughing at me, but I knows what I knows, and there are some things that ain't natural, and the Black 'Unchback and the disappearing of Sir H'Owen, and the killing of poor old Travis, is some of 'em, and I tell you frankly, sir, I'm afraid!'

It was with a very preoccupied and thoughtful look on his face that Anthony Vyne, having slipped half a crown into the old man's ready palm, strolled across the lawn with Darrell towards the house.

Pauline was standing on the edge of the grass plot talking to a tall, clean-shaven, well-built young man dressed in a suit of grey flannels, as Anthony and his friend rounded a clump of rhododendron bushes. She introduced the young man as Frank Cunningham.

'I've just been telling Frank about daddy's strange disappearance' she said, after Vyne and Cunningham had shaken hands.

'It's a most extraordinary affair, don't you think so, Mr. Vyne?' said Cunningham, in a deep pleasant voice. 'And the murder of Travis — altogether inexplicable.'

'It is probably capable of a very simple explanation,' replied the reporter. 'It has been my experience that the more uncommon and bizarre the happening, the easier it is to find a solution.'

'Let us hope that it will be so in this case,' said Cunningham. 'I suppose you haven't yet found anything in the nature of a clue?'

'Only this,' answered Anthony, and took the little golden charm from his pocket, holding it out in the palm of his hand. 'We found it clasped tightly in Travis's dead hand. It has evidently been torn from the end of a chain I suppose — why, what's the matter, man?' Vyne broke off sharply.

Frank Cunningham's face had gone ashy white, as his eyes fell on the object in Anthony's hand.

'It's impossible — impossible!' he muttered almost inaudibly. 'But, if it's true — then — It's too horrible — too horrible!'

4

The Shooter

For a moment, Anthony Vyne gazed curiously at the young man without speaking. After those few hoarsely spoken words, Cunningham had succeeded, by a prodigious effort of self-control, to master his emotions, and was rapidly becoming himself again.

Pauline laid her hand on his arm and looked up anxiously into his face, an expression of the utmost concern in her deep blue eyes.

'What's the matter, Frank?' she asked. 'Aren't you feeling well?'

Cunningham passed a slightly shaking hand across his forehead.

'I'm — I'm all right now, dear,' he answered, his voice a trifle unsteady in spite of his efforts to keep it normal. 'It was nothing — just a slight dizziness, due to the heat, I think — it's unusually hot today.'

Anthony knew that he was lying, but made no remark. At this juncture he deemed it wiser to let the incident pass without comment, but he had made up his mind to keep a watchful eye on Cunningham in future, and to tackle him upon his curious remark when a more favourable opportunity presented itself. Just at the moment he was anxious to examine the place where Pauline had found the blood marks, and where she had seen the body of her father.

He intimated this fact to Pauline, and at the reporter's request the girl led the way across the lawn to a spot about a hundred yards from the house, beside a thick shrubbery of rhododendron bushes, flanked by a narrow belt of pine trees. Here she stopped and pointed to the grass about a yard from the bushes.

'It was there, Mr. Vyne,' she said in a low voice.

Darrell followed the direction of her finger with his eyes, and saw distinctly a brownish mark staining the emerald green of the closely cut lawn, surrounded by several spots of the same ominous character.

Anthony, his head bent slightly forward, peered for some seconds intently at the blood stains. They were all that was to be seen, for the impression of the body that the girl had spoken about had long since disappeared. The natural elasticity of the grass had caused it to return to its usual appearance.

Presently Vyne allowed his gaze to wander in ever widening circles round this section of the lawn, using the blood marks as a kind of fulcrum. After a little while he commenced to walk slowly along beside the shrubbery towards the rose garden. Before he had taken more than half a dozen steps, he halted.

Almost at his feet was another stain scarcely larger than a sixpence, but clearly visible, and again, two feet away, yet another. The last was close to the bushes, almost on the edge where the grass met the dark earth, and Darrell, who had been following his friend's movements intently, saw that at this point the rhododendrons had been broken away as though by the passage of some heavy object. In several places some branches had been torn completely away.

Anthony Vyne shot a keen glance at the soft earth in which the bushes grew. Distinctly visible were the marks of a man's nailed boots. Leaving the girl and Frank Cunningham standing on the lawn, Anthony, accompanied by Darrell, forced his way gently among the thick shrubbery, taking care to avoid the footprints. Presently, following the trail of broken branches, they came to a spot where a whole bush seemed to have been broken down under some heavy weight. The green leaves were splashed all over with blood. The reporter bent forward and closely scrutinised it and the ground beneath it.

'Unless I am greatly mistaken, Jack,' he whispered softly, as he straightened up, 'this is the spot where Travis was actually killed.'

Darrell looked at his friend in astonishment.

'Actually killed!' he echoed. 'Don't you think he was shot in the Home Covert then?'

Anthony shook his head.

'I'm sure he wasn't, old chap,' he answered. 'I examined his boots, if you remember, and I found several small blades of recently cut grass adhering to the soles. There is no grass in the vicinity of the Home Covert — certainly no cut grass. No. I'm inclined to think that Travis was carried to the place where his body was found after he was dead.'

'But why, Tony?' questioned his friend. 'What for?'

'I don't know yet,' answered the reporter, and continued to search among the densely growing bushes, his sharp eyes darting hither and thither. Suddenly an exclamation from Jack Darrell caused him to look round sharply.

His friend had stopped, and was in the act of picking something up out of the soft mould.

'What have you found?' asked Anthony quickly.

'This,' answered Darrell, and handed him a little brass cylinder.

Vyne looked at the cartridge case, and nodded thoughtfully.

'A .35 Automatic,' he remarked in a

low tone. 'I knew that the bullet that killed Travis was nickel jacketed by the wound it made. Come on, let's see if there's anything else.'

They moved on slowly, closely examining every inch of the ground around them. From the broken bush a second trail of footprints led away among the pine trees. Vyne dropped on to one knee, and peered closely at one that was more clearly defined than the rest.

'There is not the shadow of a doubt that these prints were made by Travis, which confirms my theory that the crime was actually committed here,' he said. 'You see where part of the sole has become loose and left a characteristic mark. It is identical with the sole of one of the boots that the gamekeeper was wearing at the time of his death.'

He rose to his feet, and as he did so he suddenly caught sight of a small object half hidden under a bush a few paces away. Crossing over to it he picked it up, turning it about in his hands, while a queer little smile curled the corners of his lips.

Darrell hurried to his side, and inspected the object in his friend's hand. It was a large .35 Automatic pistol. Anthony jerked back the cover and examined the contents of the magazine. One shell had been ejected! At the same time Darrell caught sight of some marks that had been scratched on the butt. He drew his companion's attention to them, and Vyne looked more closely. They were the initials O.L. roughly engraved.

'Owen Langley,' murmured Anthony quietly.

'Good Heavens!' gasped his friend, as a sudden thought entered his mind. 'Surely it can't have been Sir Owen who shot Travis?'

Vyne made no answer, but continued to stare thoughtfully at the pistol, his brows wrinkled in a puzzled frown. Presently he came back to his present surroundings with a start, put the pistol in his pocket, and continued his search among the shrubbery. They found nothing else, however, and shortly returned to where they had left Cunningham and the girl.

'Have you found anything, Mr. Vyne?' she asked eagerly, as the reporter and Darrell re-joined her.

Anthony put his hand in his pocket and produced the pistol.

'Do you recognise that, Miss Langley?' he asked, holding it out to her.

Pauline looked at it, suppressing a slight shudder as she did so.

'Why, yes,' she replied at length. 'It belonged to daddy. If you look, you will see his initials on the butt. Where did you find it?'

Vyne explained briefly, omitting, however, to mention about the footprints of the gamekeeper.

'Daddy must have taken it with him when he came out last night,' she remarked. 'Mr. Vyne, what do you think has happened to him?'

Anthony looked at her gravely.

'I really cannot say at present,' he answered, 'although I don't think you need have any reason to be alarmed. I don't believe that Sir Owen is in any danger.'

They had turned, and were all four slowly making their way across the lawn in the direction of the house. Cunningham was walking beside the girl, but presently he gradually dropped behind, and drew near to Anthony who was slightly in the rear. While Jack Darrell was talking to Pauline, and her attention was momentarily distracted, he touched the reporter's arm and leant towards him.

'I am leaving almost at once, Mr. Vyne,' he whispered; 'I wish you would walk part of the way back to the village with me. I have something I wish to say to you.'

Anthony glanced quickly up at the troubled face so close to his own and nodded.

At that moment the girl finished her conversation with Darrell, and turned.

'You'll stay to lunch, won't you, Frank?' she asked, as they passed close to the house. Cunningham shook his head.

'No, dear, if you'll excuse me,' he answered. 'There are one or two things I must attend to. I'll come back later on, though,' he added, as he saw the disappointment in the girl's eyes.

'I'll walk a little way with you,' interposed Vyne. 'What time do you lunch, Miss Langley?'

Pauline glanced at the little gold watch on her wrist.

'In about half an hour,' she replied; 'don't be late.'

'No, don't be late, old chap,' said Darrell; 'I'm as hungry as three people already.'

'Don't let him get anywhere near the kitchen then, Miss Langley,' advised Anthony, smiling, 'or there won't be any lunch for the rest of us.'

Cunningham said goodbye to the girl, and a moment later they were striding along a narrow country lane towards the village.

For some minutes they walked in silence, which was presently broken by Cunningham.

'Mr. Vyne,' he began haltingly, 'I hope you will treat what I am going to tell you in strict confidence.'

'I'm afraid I can't promise that,' answered Anthony. 'If it has any bearing at all on the death of Travis, and is likely to be of assistance in tracing his murderer, it is plainly my duty to put it at the disposal of the police.'

The young man was silent, and it was plain to Vyne that he was turning over the reporter's words in his mind, and trying to decide upon his course of action. After a pause, he continued: 'Of course, Mr. Vyne, you are perfectly right, but I feel that I must tell someone, and afterwards you must act as you think fit. Who do you think killed Travis?'

He jerked out the last question like a shot from a gun, and then before Anthony had time to make a reply, he went on rapidly: 'You must have thought I was mad when I behaved as I did at the sight of that gold charm, but it gave me an awful shock. You see, I'd seen it before, and I knew to whom it belonged.'

Vyne looked up at Cunningham's excited face, a glint of interest in his eyes.

'Whom did it belong to?' he asked.

'Sir Owen,' replied the young man rapidly. 'You can realise what a shock it was to me when you stated that it had been found in Travis's hand. I hope to heaven I'm wrong, but everything seems to point to the fact that it was Sir Owen who shot Travis. It is the only reason I can see to account for his strange disappearance. And then the pistol — that also belonged to Sir Owen. Certainly, it wasn't found near the scene of the murder, but he might easily have thrown it away later, and but for you it might never have been found at all. If it should prove that my suspicion is correct, it will be terrible for Pauline, far worse than anything that could happen!'

Anthony remained silent for several minutes before he replied. Then he said quietly: 'I believe at the time of Sir Owen's disappearance he was dressed in pyjamas and a dressing gown — wasn't he?'

Cunningham gazed at him blankly.

'I don't quite follow you,' he said. 'You're perfectly right, but what has that got to do with the point we are discussing?'

'Only, doesn't it strike you as curious,' replied Anthony, 'that a man dressed in that way should be wearing any sort of ornament at all?'

The young man stopped in his walk, and his face lightened.

'By Jove! You're right!' he exclaimed. 'What an idiot I am not to have thought of that. Then Sir Owen didn't — ?'

'Wait,' interposed Vyne. 'I'm not saying that it is impossible for Sir Owen to have killed Travis because of that. I am only pointing out that the reason on which you based your suspicions was not a sound one.'

Cunningham's face clouded again as he resumed his walk.

'Then you think he did kill him?' he asked gloomily.

Anthony shook his head with a slight smile.

'I think neither one way nor the other at present,' he replied. 'Why was it that Miss Langley didn't recognise the charm as belonging to her father?' he continued, after a slight pause.

'I doubt if she ever saw it,' said Cunningham, 'or if she did, she didn't remember it. It used to be open on Sir Owen's desk in the library, and Pauline seldom went in there.'

'He didn't habitually wear it then?' asked Vyne.

'He never wore it as far as I know,' replied Cunningham.

'I wonder if it could have been the same one,' mused the detective. 'They must be fairly common — most masons wear one.'

'Oh, I'm certain it was the same one,' said the young man emphatically. 'It is impossible to mistake that piece of chain to which it is attached. You must have noticed the peculiar formation of the links — like four-pointed stars.'

Vyne nodded, he had noticed that very fact. It seemed that there could be little doubt that the gold charm was the property of Sir Owen Langley.

They had come by now to a cross road, and here Frank Cunningham halted.

'If you don't want to be late for lunch, you'd better be getting back, Mr. Vyne,' he said, as he glanced at his watch. 'You'll just about do it, I think. I live along here.' He pointed to the right of the intersecting road. 'It was very good of you to have listened to my nonsense, but I can assure you that it was troubling me a great deal. Although I am still by no means easy in my mind I feel ever so much better for having got it off my chest. I suppose I shall see you later?'

He shook hands almost cheerfully with Anthony and they parted.

The reporter felt in his pocket for his cigarette case, and having selected and lighted one, strolled back along the leafy country road, turning over in his mind the main points of the problem on which he was engaged. Could it be possible that Sir Owen's was the hand that had caused the gamekeeper's death? And that it was for this reason that he had disappeared? In that case, whose had been the body that Pauline had seen lying upon the lawn wrapped in her father's dressing gown, and also what was the meaning of the mysterious figure in black whom she insisted she had seen bending over it?

Then, again, there was the old gardener's story. Travis himself had apparently seen this same figure some three days before his death, therefore it could hardly be a figment of the girl's imagination. And the treasure, too. Was that merely a side issue that had nothing whatever to do with the case, or had it its allotted place in the scheme of things?

According to Pauline's story, Sir Owen had taken the legend of the treasure and the Black Hunchback seriously, and had succeeded in finding a clue to the hiding place, and from that time the whole series of events had commenced. Was this merely a coincidence? Vyne was inclined to think it was not. The whole affair was like an elaborate jig-saw puzzle. All the pieces lay scattered about, but try as he would Anthony could not make them fit into a coherent whole. Indeed, he was not even certain that he held all the pieces.

With a little exclamation of impatience he stopped, threw away the butt of his cigarette and lighted another. At the same moment there came a sharp crack from the leafy screen that bordered the road on the right, and Anthony Vyne ducked sharply as a bullet whizzed past his head and buried itself with a dull thud in a tree trunk behind him!

5

A Cry in the Night!

After that one shot all was silent again save for the ordinary sounds of the country side. Eight feet of gravel bank bordered the side of the road from which the shot had come, and on the top of this a wire fence. Beyond this fence was thick woodland, the trees growing close up to the side of the road. Anthony Vyne knew that if he kept close to this bank, the unknown marksman would be unable to reach him.

His first inclination had been to climb the bank, and try to discover if possible the identity of his assailant, but a moment's thought had shown him the futility of such a course. For one thing in doing so he would be making himself an excellent target for the other's shots, and for another it would be next to impossible to trace anyone in those dense woods, so

Anthony contented himself with keeping out of range, and proceeded on his way back to Langley Towers.

The bullet, as near as he had been able to judge by the sound, had struck the tree trunk on the opposite side of the road somewhere near the base, and this, taken in conjunction with the fact that the upper ground in the wood was eight feet higher than the road level, led the reporter to the conclusion that the shot had been fired from a high elevation — possibly the shooter, whoever it was, had fired from a tree. As to his identity — if he it were — Vyne couldn't hazard a guess. The whole thing was mysterious and inexplicable, only one thing was certain — someone was extremely anxious to stop his enquiries into the disappearance of Sir Owen Langley and the murder of the gamekeeper.

But Vyne had been put on his guard, and he made a firm resolve that he would not be caught napping in future. This time the mysterious assailant had had it all his own way and had very nearly succeeded in his object, because his attack had been a complete surprise. But not only had he failed in his purpose, he had shown his hand, and Anthony believed in the old adage that 'Forewarned is forearmed.'

Nothing further occurred during his walk back to the Towers, and he arrived five minutes late for lunch, and found Darrell almost speechless with indignation.

'It's too bad,' the fat man complained as he entered the room. 'I'm almost on the verge of collapse from starvation, and you stroll in as if there was no such thing as food in existence.'

'Half the joy of life is in anticipation,' said Vyne smiling.

'I wish you'd thought of that sooner, and been five minutes early instead of five minutes late,' retorted Jack, as he commenced an attack on his soup.

Anthony made no reference to his adventure during the meal, keeping the conversation as much as possible to light and trifling matters, and avoiding all mention of the case on which he was engaged.

The girl seemed to have recovered some of her spirits although she was far from happy, and altogether it was quite a pleasant meal.

After lunch, Pauline excused herself to attend to some household duties, and Vyne and Darrell found themselves alone. The reporter suggested a stroll in the grounds, and after some persuasion his friend agreed and presently found themselves amid the riotous colours and glorious perfume of the rose garden. Anthony recounted his conversation with Frank Cunningham, concluding with the story of his experience on the return journey.

'Gee!' exclaimed Jack, his small eyes shining with excitement. 'It looks as if we've struck it this time with a vengeance.'

'It certainly is a most puzzling case, old chap,' agreed Anthony.

'Do you think Cunningham's suspicions are right?' asked Darrell, 'and that it was Sir Owen who shot Travis?'

'To be perfectly candid,' replied Anthony, 'I don't know what to think. I'm as completely mystified as you are. But supposing Sir Owen was responsible for the death of the gamekeeper, what possible motive could he have in killing him? Besides, that doesn't explain the presence of the other figure — the dwarfish shape which Miss Langley swears she saw bending over her father on the lawn, and which was also seen by Travis on another occasion, or the interesting person who tried to put a bullet through me in the lane.'

'Unless it was Sir Owen,' suggested his friend quietly.

Vyne shot a sudden glance at him.

'What exactly do you mean?' he asked.

'I've been thinking,' replied Darrell. 'Sir Owen was interested in the legend of the Black Hunchback. Supposing that for some reason he wished to be able to come and go at night without being seen and recognised by anyone. What is more natural than that he should hit on the idea of disguising himself as the family ghost? Even if anyone did see him, they would be too scared to enquire into his identity very closely. And supposing during one of his nocturnal excursions, he had been recognised by Travis, and shot him to prevent him giving the game away.'

'But why should he disappear afterwards?' asked Anthony, as Darrell stopped for breath. 'There would have been nothing to connect him with the gamekeeper's death.'

'He got scared,' answered Darrell promptly. 'Probably he shot Travis on the spur of the moment, and was afraid to stay and face the possible consequences.'

Anthony shook his head slowly.

'I'm afraid, old chap, you've let your imagination run away with you,' he said. 'You forget that Miss Langley saw the figure of the Black Hunchback approaching the house across the lawn before she heard her father's bedroom door open, and don't forget a most important point, she heard two shots, not one. No, Jack, I think we shall find that the solution to the mystery is far more subtle and far more complicated than that.'

Darrell looked up at his friend curiously; something in the reporter's tone had given him the idea that Vyne knew or guessed more than he had said. He made no remark, however, and Anthony relapsed into a thoughtful silence which remained unbroken until, having completed their stroll round the rose garden, they were returning across the lawn to the house. Then, as if speaking his thoughts aloud, Anthony broke the silence.

'If I were you, Jack,' he murmured softly, 'I should try and get a bit of a rest this afternoon if you can. I'm inclined to think that there will be further developments tonight, and you'll feel fresher.'

'Why, what do you think is going to happen?' asked the stout man excitedly.

'I don't know,' replied Vyne candidly, 'but I've got a feeling — call it intuition if you like — that the Black Hunchback will be abroad again tonight, and I for one don't intend to miss the chance of getting a glimpse of him.'

At that moment a servant appeared from the house, and was apparently looking for them, for as soon as he caught sight of Anthony Vyne he hurried in the reporter's direction.

'Inspector Hallam is on the telephone, sir,' he announced as he came up to them.

'I'll come at once,' said Vyne, and hurried after the man with Darrell panting as his heels.

The telephone stood in the spacious hall of the Towers, and in a few minutes Anthony was listening to the gruff voice of Detective Inspector Hallam.

'That you, Vyne?' it said. 'I've been trying to get you for some time. I 'phoned up your flat first, and Frost told me where you were.'

'What's the trouble, Hallam?' asked Anthony, as the Inspector paused.

'North,' was the brief reply, and there was a touch of bitterness in the single syllable. 'Disappeared completely, and has been missing for several days. When we went up to execute the warrant, this morning, on your advice, we found the bird had flown.'

'But surely you had been having him watched!' said the reporter incredulously.

There was the sound of a cough at the other end of the wire.

'Well — er — no, I didn't think it was necessary. You see, we thought it was a plain case of suicide with Old Harper until you suggested the poison. That put a different aspect on the case, of course,'

— there was a pause, then — 'I say, Vyne, can you do anything? I shall get a frightful roasting from the Chief over this.'

'What do you want me to do?' asked Anthony. 'Find North?'

'Well, if you could lend a hand, I'd be awfully pleased, old chap,' answered Hallam. 'Of course, we've got all the usual lines going, but if you could do anything — '

'All right, old man,' said Anthony, 'I'll do my best, but at the moment I'm fairly busy. I'll try and get up to the Yard tomorrow and see you.' He rang off and hung up the receiver!

'What's up?' asked Darrell, who had been standing by. 'What did old Hallam want?'

'North has got away,' answered his friend, and recounted the Inspector's conversation over the telephone. 'Of course, it's not Hallam's fault,' he went on; 'there wasn't a shadow of suspicion against the man until I suggested that the glass might have contained poison, and they found it had. I suspected him from the beginning, as soon as I was convinced that it was not a case of suicide. The mere fact of his disappearance is conclusive proof of his guilt. If possible I shall run up to town and see Hallam tomorrow.'

The case which Anthony referred to had appeared at first sight a particularly simple one. Old Jonathan Harper, a dealer in precious stones, had been found shot in his flat in Bloomsbury. The pistol had been found in his hand, and it had seemed a clear case of suicide until Vyne, acting for *The Messenger* had proved conclusively that the old man had not died from the effect of the bullet but from poison, the shot having been fired after his death. North had been staying with Harper, and had only moved, after the old man's death, to a fresh lodging and from here, according to Hallam, he had disappeared. In some way or other, he must have got wind of the police suspicions, and fled.

After the worthy Inspector's message, Vyne and Darrell parted, the stout man taking his friend's advice, sought his room and lay down, although it was a long time before his active brain allowed him to drop into a doze. He kept turning over and over in his mind the facts of the case, and tried vainly to find a solution that would fit them all.

Anthony, left to himself, made his way into the library, and after a short search discovered the old manuscript containing a detailed account of the hiding of the treasure and the legend of the Black Hunchback that Pauline had told him about.

For the remainder of the afternoon the reporter pored over this and found it remarkably interesting. It contained several facts that the girl had omitted to mention, or had failed to remember, in her short account of the story, although there was nothing that gave even the slightest clue to the place where the treasure had been hidden. It was true that there was a copy of the doggerel verse which was supposed to contain the secret of the hiding place, but although Anthony spent some considerable time in closely studying it; he was no wiser by the time he had finished than when he started.

As it drew near to tea-time, he heard

Frank Cunningham's voice talking to Pauline on the lawn, and presently the reporter put away the manuscript and joined them. When tea was served on the terrace there was no sign of Darrell, and the maid reported that the stout man was not in his room. About halfway through the meal, however, Darrell appeared, and Vyne could see that he was full of suppressed excitement.

There was a sparkle in his small eyes that his friend knew of old. Darrell said nothing, however, and Anthony made no comment, and it was not until later when they were dressing for dinner that Darrell found a chance of speaking to his friend alone. Anthony was in the act of tying his tie, when Jack came into his room.

'I say,' he burst out at once, 'I've got something to tell you.' Anthony patted the ends of his bow into place, 'I knew you had,' he replied, smiling. 'Come on, what is it?'

Darrell seated himself on the side of the bed, and it creaked in protest under his weight.

'Old Hume, the butler, is secretly supplying food to someone outside the house,' he announced.

Anthony Vyne swung round sharply.

'How do you know that?' he rapped quickly.

'I saw him,' answered his friend. 'After I had been sleeping for about an hour, I woke, and it looked so tempting outside that I decided to go for a stroll before tea. I found myself, presently, in the kitchen garden. From there you can see into the kitchen and a light was burning. I suppose it's rather dark and they keep a light on most of the time. The kitchen was empty except for the butler, and I should have passed on without taking any further notice if his actions had not caught my attention. He was engaged in packing a quantity of food into a basket, and as I watched he fetched two bottles and put them in with the rest, and also some cigarettes. Just at that moment one of the other servants entered the kitchen, and Hume hastily concealed the basket under the table. He wouldn't have done that if everything had been open and above board.'

Anthony was listening intently, a little glimmer of elation in his eyes.

'It's certainly peculiar, old chap,' he commented softly. 'We must find out the destination of that basket.'

'It rather bears out my idea about Sir Owen, doesn't it, Tony?' said Jack.

'You think he's going to take it to Sir Owen?' asked Anthony.

'I do,' he replied; 'don't you?'

His friend paused before replying.

'In that case, Sir Owen must have taken the old man into his confidence.'

'Well, why not?' asked Darrell. 'These old family servants are generally devoted to their masters, and would do anything for them. I don't think it's such a wild idea.'

'But what about his daughter?' said Anthony. 'Surely, it would be far more natural for Sir Owen to make a confidante of her than of a servant, however trusting he may be. Besides, he must know that she is naturally anxious about him.'

'I don't know, Anthony,' argued Darrell. 'If Sir Owen was responsible for the death of Travis, and if he had been doing something that wasn't particularly to his credit, he'd scarcely want his daughter to know, would he?'

Anthony smiled.

'You're still clinging to that theory then?' he asked.

'I don't see any other,' answered Darrell. 'The more I think of it the more it seems to me that Sir Owen is at the bottom of the whole thing. After all, Miss Langley may have been mistaken about the shadow bending over her father. Moonlight plays peculiar tricks at times, and my theory covers all the facts.'

'It doesn't account for the person who shot at me,' murmured the detective.

'I think it was Sir Owen,' said Jack stubbornly; 'If I'm right and he was engaged on some underhand game, he would naturally get the wind up at the thought that you were investigating the case, and become fearful lest you should discover the truth.'

'You may be right,' said Anthony as he slipped on his dinner jacket, 'and it's not a bad theory anyhow. But I personally don't think it's the right one. One thing, however, is certain. Hume must not be allowed to leave the house with that basket unless he is followed, and that's where you come in, old man. If he's conveying it to some secret destination, and from your account of his behaviour I don't think there is much doubt of that, he won't attempt to do so while it remains light, and there's a risk of his being seen.'

During dinner, Anthony kept a watchful eye upon the old butler, and although Hume performed his duties in the deft and silent manner that only an old servant with years of practice can attain, the reporter noticed a strained and anxious look in the old man's face that spoke plainly of some secret worry, but which Vyne would scarcely have seen if he had not been specially looking for something of the sort.

Young Cunningham stayed to dinner, and afterwards the four of them adjourned to the billiard room and played snooker.

Pauline, unlike most women, was an adept at the game, and in partnership with Anthony, easily beat the other two. They continued to play until Cunningham announced his intention of going home. After the young man had departed, they remained talking for a while in the drawing room.

Darrell and the girl were arguing over a

rule in the game they had just played, and Anthony allowed his eyes to wander round the pretty tastefully furnished room. They rested at last on the mantelpiece. It contained, among other things, the portrait of a particularly beautiful woman, almost a girl, in a silver frame, and Anthony Vyne thought as he gazed at it that he had seldom seen such a perfect face. The old-fashioned dress she was wearing dated the picture, and it must have been taken many years previously.

Pauline looked up and caught the direction of the reporter's glance.

'That was daddy's first wife,' she said, as if in answer to Anthony's silent question. 'She must have been very beautiful.'

Vyne agreed.

'I'd no idea that Sir Owen had been married twice,' he remarked.

'Very few people know,' answered the girl. 'Daddy seldom spoke about it. He was very young when the marriage took place, and I believe she died a year after. I don't think he ever really forgot her,' she went on sadly, 'for although mother and he were very happy, I don't think he ever loved her in the same way as his first wife.'

She continued her conversation with Darrell, and Anthony sat silent, thinking over the fresh fact he had just learned.

Very shortly after, they broke up for the night, and as Vyne and Darrell reached the landing on which their rooms were situated, the reporter pressed his friend's arm.

'Slip into another suit,' he whispered, 'and then come back into my room.'

Jack nodded, and hurried away.

Anthony entered his own bedroom and proceeded leisurely to undress and don an old tweed suit over which he slipped his dressing gown, then he unlocked his suitcase, and searched in its interior. In a few seconds he found what he wanted, a roll of what looked like fine rope made of silk. When he shook it out, it proved to be a beautifully made ladder. Vyne seldom travelled without this, for on more than one occasion he had proved its worth. He crossed to the window and flung it open, and just as he did so the door opened and Darrell entered the room.

The stout man had changed, and seeing

Anthony drop the end of the ladder out the window, went to his friend's assistance without a word. Working swiftly they soon secured the steel hooks with which one end of the ladder was provided, to the inner side of the sill, and Vyne carefully tested them. They seemed firm enough, and with an exclamation of satisfaction the reporter leaned out of the open window. It was a brilliant moonlight night, and Anthony could easily see the end of the ladder. It reached to within a foot or two of the ground.

Quickly he pulled it up again, and coiled it on the sill.

'That forms a quick method of getting out,' he remarked, as he pulled down the blind and turned from the window. He had not switched on the light, undressing by the moonlight which flooded the room, but now he crossed to the switch and pressed it down.

'We'll turn it out in a minute or two, old boy, and that will give anyone watching the impression that we've gone to bed. Not that I imagine that there's anyone about yet. It's too early. You put your light out before you came in, I suppose?' Jack nodded.

'What do you really expect to happen?' he asked.

'I haven't the least idea,' answered Anthony, 'but I shall be very surprised if the night passes without a diversion of some kind. But don't talk — sound carries in a place like this, and I don't want to advertise the fact that we are up.'

Darrell relapsed into silence, and presently Vyne signed to him to turn off the light. He did so, and the reporter cautiously raised the blind, then drawing an armchair close to the open window, he settled himself down among the cushions.

'I should lie down if I were you,' he advised in a whisper. 'I'll call you if anything happens.'

Nothing loath, Darrell obeyed him, and the reporter sat on motionless, his eyes fixed on the moon-bathed garden. The slight breeze which had sprung up at sunset blew gently in at the open window, bringing with it a delicious perfume from the rose garden. Everything was very still and peaceful.

After a while the sound of heavy, regular breathing from the direction of the bed told Anthony that Darrell had fallen asleep, and he smiled quietly.

Twelve o'clock struck from the deep toned clock in the hall, then one, and still the tranquil silence of the night remained unbroken.

Anthony must have dropped into a slight doze, for the clock striking two awoke him with a start. He sat up sharply in his chair, and at the same instant there rang through the silent house a scream laden with terror.

'Help! Help!' shrieked a woman's voice. 'Mr. Vyne! Help!'

And the voice was that of Pauline Langley!

6

The Hut in the Wood

Anthony was out of his chair like a streak of lightning, and flinging open the door dashed out into the dark corridor outside. In a second he had pressed down the switch, the position of which he had carefully noted before retiring, and flooded the place with light.

Pauline's room was on the same floor at the end of the corridor, and Vyne went racing along towards her door.

He tried the handle. It was locked! Without wasting a second he let fly with the flat of his foot just over the lock, and with a splintering crash the door flew open. The reporter's fingers searched for the switch and flashed on the light.

The girl was sitting up in bed, her eyes round with horror, her hand clutching at her throat.

'What happened?' rapped Anthony

sharply. 'What made you cry out?'

Still fingering her throat with one hand, Pauline pointed with the other towards the window without speaking. It was wide open, and the reporter could see the top of a ladder resting against the sill.

In a second he was at the window and looking out. A figure was hurrying across the lawn in the moonlight, a squat misshapen dwarfish figure dressed in black. A thrill ran through Anthony's veins as he looked — the Black Hunchback!

Without hesitation he flung his legs over the sill and started to descend the ladder. The Thing was already entering the shadow of the shrubbery.

Almost sliding down the ladder in his haste, Vyne reached the ground, and raced in pursuit. From the shadow of the bushes came a sharp crack and a bullet whizzed past his ear. He could hear the sound of something forcing its way through the shrubbery.

Anthony felt in his pockets for his automatic, and realised with a sharp pang of disappointment that he had left it in his bedroom. Still nothing daunted, he kept on.

The noise of breaking branches had ceased, and all was still. Vyne reached the edge of the shrubbery and stopped to listen.

Cautiously, for he had no desire to expose himself needlessly to the fire of the unknown's automatic, he slipped out of his dressing gown, and wormed his way through the dense bushes at the point where it had been entered by the marauder. The passage taken by the other was plainly visible by the torn and broken branches. Vyne followed this trail until presently it emerged from the shrubbery into a small clearing in which stood a large and massive oak, but all sign of the intruder had vanished. With a feeling of chagrin, Anthony turned to retrace his steps. It was useless carrying the pursuit any further, particularly as he was unarmed and would stand little chance against the other's weapon.

Slipping on his dressing gown again, he walked slowly back towards the house. The cries and the shot had aroused the rest of the household, and Vyne entered by the side door which was opened by Hume.

Anthony noted, with a slight thrill, that the old man was fully dressed! The reporter made his way as quickly as possible to Pauline's bedroom, and here he found Darrell and the housekeeper, Mrs. Wakefield.

She was holding a bottle of smelling salts to the girl's nostrils as Anthony entered.

'What exactly happened, Miss Langley?' he asked as he crossed to the bed.

The girl pushed back her hair with a trembling hand.

'Oh, it was dreadful!' she said in a weak trembling voice. 'I've never been so frightened before in my life. If you'd seen that awful figure — without a face — ' She broke off, shuddering, and the kindly old housekeeper patted her hand soothingly.

'I fell asleep almost directly I lay down,' she went on, 'and then suddenly it seemed as if I couldn't breathe, and I woke. A horrible shapeless, dwarfish figure was bending over me and pressing something against my mouth. I tore it away and screamed for you, and the Thing ran to the window and climbed out.'

'I found this by the side of the bed,' interposed Darrell, holding out a white object.

Anthony Vyne took it from his friend's hand. It was a pad of cotton wool and reeked with a sickly smell that resembled stale apples.

'Humph! Chloroform!' muttered the reporter in a low tone.

'Did you see anything?' asked Darrell eagerly. Vyne nodded absently.

'I saw our friend — whoever it was,' he replied. 'I very nearly felt him as well. That's the second time he's almost put a bullet through me, and it was too close to be pleasant.'

'What does it all mean, Mr. Vyne?' asked the frightened girl.

'That's what I'm going to find out,' said Anthony grimly. 'I'm beginning to get a hazy idea. I should advise you to try and get some sleep, Miss Langley. I don't think you have anything else to fear tonight, but as a precaution get Mrs. Wakefield to spend the rest of the night with you. Come on, old chap,' he added to Darrell. 'We might also try and get some rest; we shall have a heavy day before us tomorrow.'

They returned along the passage to their rooms.

'Well, what do you make of it, Anthony?' enquired the stout man as they paused outside their respective rooms.

'It rather upsets your theory of Sir Owen being at the bottom of the mystery, doesn't it?' evaded Vyne. 'He would scarcely be likely to try and chloroform his own daughter.'

'Yes, I suppose that's true enough,' agreed Jack. 'But who was it, and what possible motive could they have?'

'No more questions now,' said Anthony as he opened his door. 'I'm going to bed.'

But he didn't. Hunched up in an armchair in his dressing gown, a cigarette between his lips, and an open box near his hand, he smoked and thought all through the rest of the night, and the sun was streaming in through the open window before he finally rose and made his way to the bathroom.

* * *

Anthony breakfasted early and alone. The shock of the night's events, combined with the loss of sleep, had kept Pauline confined to her room, and she sent a word of apology to the reporter by Mrs. Wakefield.

Vyne was not sorry. The solitary meal gave him an opportunity for thought, and he had plenty to occupy his mind.

The mysterious attack upon the girl had been totally unexpected. He had been prepared for a visit from the Black Hunchback, but the form it had taken had mystified him completely.

What could be the object of the unknown's interest in the girl? It was obvious that abduction had been in the intruder's mind, as witness the chloroform pad, but rack his brains as he might, Anthony could not find the very faintest trace of a motive. The whole affair, from the disappearance of Sir Owen and the murder of the gamekeeper, to this last development, appeared absolutely inexplicable.

At the back of the reporter's mind, however, was a certainty that, forming the hub as it were of the whole mystery, was the treasure.

He was convinced that it was more than a coincidence that the whole train of preceding events had started from the moment that Sir Owen was supposed to have discovered the clue to the whereabouts of the hidden bullion. Now, who, besides Pauline, had been aware of this fact?

Vyne determined to get Darrell to make enquiries and find out from the girl. In all probability the entire household knew, for apparently it had been no secret that Sir Owen had been working for years on the clue provided by old Sir Hugo Lang.

The reporter had finished his breakfast, and was just inhaling the first puff of his cigarette, when Darrell appeared.

'Good morning,' said the fat man cheerily, as he seated himself at the table. 'I hope you haven't wolfed all the grub, for I'm as hungry as the fasting man in a circus after a continuous performance.'

Anthony smiled.

'It appears to be a chronic complaint with you, old chap,' he replied. 'However, I think you will find sufficient to keep the pangs of hunger away for an hour or so on the sideboard.'

Darrell grabbed a plate with alacrity, and crossing to the sideboard commenced to pile it with kidneys and bacon from the chafing dish.

'Well, what's the programme today?' he asked as he returned to the table, and commenced to attack his breakfast.

'I'm going to run up to town to see Hallam,' said his friend, 'so you will be left to your own devices. Don't get into any trouble if you can help it, and keep a sharp eye on Hume. I am particularly anxious to learn the destination of that basket of food. I'm certain that he has not had an opportunity of leaving the house with it as yet. I believe he intended doing so last night, but the disturbance caused by the visit of our unknown friend prevented him. However, I think he'll make another attempt as soon as ever he thinks the coast is clear, and that's where you come in.'

‘I’ll hang on to him like a leech,’ said Jack, reaching across for some more toast.

‘Whatever you do, don’t let him suspect he is being watched,’ warned Vyne, dropping the stub of his cigarette into the ashtray. ‘It might spoil everything.’

‘You can trust me,’ replied his friend, with his mouth now full of bacon. ‘What time will you be back?’

‘I hope to get back in time for dinner.’ Anthony rose to his feet. ‘Another thing, my lad, try and find out from Miss Langley who, besides herself, knows that her father had succeeded in discovering the hiding place of the treasure.’

Darrell looked up quickly at the reporter.

‘You think then that the treasure is at the bottom of the mystery?’ he asked.

Anthony nodded.

‘I’m convinced that the whole affair turns on it,’ he answered quietly. He glanced at his watch. ‘I must be off now. Goodbye, old chap,’ he announced.

‘Give my love to old Hallam,’ cried Darrell flippantly.

Halfway to the door, Anthony paused. 'One last word before I go,' he said gravely. 'On no account is Miss Langley to leave the house after dusk! You understand, on no excuse whatever. Her life may depend on her obeying my instructions.'

With a brief farewell, he left the room, and Jack Darrell continued to eat his breakfast in thoughtful silence.

Having finished his breakfast, he strolled out into the grounds. It was a perfect summer morning. A cool gentle breeze had sprung up during the night, and it dissipated to a marked extent the intense heat of the sun.

It seemed almost impossible to associate the gently waving branches of the trees and the perfume and brilliant colouring of the flowers, with the dark and sinister shadow which had taken up its abode around Langley Towers. The whole thing viewed in the light of day seemed to be part of some fantastic nightmare, and Darrell had to exercise all his imagination to convince himself that it was indeed a reality.

A cheery 'hello' caused him to turn as

he was crossing the lawn, and he saw Frank Cunningham coming towards him.

The young man had, of course, heard nothing of the events of the previous night, and he greeted Jack with a cheery good-morning.

'I didn't expect to find anyone up yet,' he remarked as they strolled together across the fresh emerald grass. 'But I couldn't sleep very well last night — worrying about this infernal mystery — so I thought I'd come over and see if there had been any further developments.'

In spite of his cheerful demeanour, the young man looked haggard, and there were dark marks under his eyes.

He listened gravely as the stout man related what had occurred during the night.

'But this is getting terrible,' he cried when Jack had finished.' Why in the world should anyone try and kidnap Pauline? What does Mr. Vyne think of it all?'

'You never know what Anthony thinks until he's ready for you to know,' replied Jack, 'and that's when he's got the whole thing worked out. He hates saying anything until he's got proof that his theory is correct.'

'You're sure she wasn't hurt at all?' enquired Cunningham.

Darrell shook his head. 'No, there wasn't time,' he replied. 'Of course, she's had a bit of a shock, but a rest will soon put her right.'

'I think I'll go and see Mrs. Wakefield,' said Cunningham, 'and find out when it will be possible to see Pauline. So long, old man! See you later.'

He strode off towards the house, and Darrell stood watching his tall figure as he crossed the sunlit lawn. There was a puzzled frown on the stout man's cheery face. It almost seemed as though Cunningham had expected to hear that something had happened during the night, hence his early visit. Certainly he had not slept, the dark marks under his eyes betrayed that fact.

Darrell's thoughts concerning Frank Cunningham were suddenly switched off in another direction. From where he stood, through a long gap in the shrubbery of rhododendron bushes that bordered the lawn, he could see part of the kitchen garden, and crossing this he suddenly descried the figure of the old butler, Hume!

The old man was dressed as usual, but was wearing a soft hat, and a thrill ran through Darrell's heart as he noted that he carried under one arm, a large brown paper parcel!

Could this be the contents of the basket that he had seen the butler packing on the previous day, put up into more convenient form? Surely the old man would hardly choose broad daylight to carry the food to its destination. But then Darrell remembered that he had been, according to Anthony's idea, prevented from leaving the house during the night by the alarm caused by the visit of the mysterious marauder. In all probability the matter was urgent, and he was taking the first opportunity that his duties would allow of leaving the house, and had chosen this hour — it was barely half past seven — as being the safest. At any rate, Jack was taking no risks and decided to follow the man.

Hume had passed out of sight behind the bushes, but Darrell guessed that he was making for a little gate at the bottom of the kitchen garden that led out into a narrow lane, and later joined the main road which led to the village.

The stout man hurried down the steps into the rose garden. His object was to slip through into the Home Covert. Alongside that ran a wood leading into the lane down which the butler would have to travel, it being the only exit from the kitchen garden without crossing the lawn.

Old Edwards, the gardener, was busy at work in one corner among his beloved roses, and Darrell, knowing the old man's talkative nature, hurried round on the other side to avoid him. The door leading to the Home Covert stood ajar, and he slipped through, making his way quickly among the thickly growing trees to the edge of the wood where it bordered on the lane.

Concealed behind the shielding screen of a massive tree trunk he peered cautiously out into the narrow roadway. The figure of the old butler had passed through the little gate, and was about half way down the lane going in the direction of the main road. Jack Darrell followed, still keeping in the shadow of the trees, and taking care to step warily to avoid any sound from the rotting undergrowth. It was impossible to risk the lane itself. It offered no cover, and the old man had only to turn his head to become aware instantly of his shadower.

Hume certainly didn't appear to be in any hurry. Leisurely he ambled down the steep incline of the leafy lane, every now and again darting a sharp glance behind him and to right and left. Evidently he was making sure that he was not being followed.

Darrell chuckled to himself as he slipped softly along in the other's wake, noiseless as a shadow, and not nearly so visible. At the juncture where the little byeway met the main road, Hume halted for a moment to remove his hat and wipe the perspiration from his forehead, then turning to the right, set off towards the village.

Now came Darrell's big risk. In order to follow the butler, he had to forsake the friendly cover offered by the little wood and come out into the open. The road down which Hume was making his way offered not a vestige of concealment of any kind. Bordered on either side by a strip of grass beyond which, on the left, was a broad ditch, the road ran in almost a straight line dipping sharply towards the village. Away on the right rose the wooded slopes of the Chiltern Hills, sharply defined in the clear morning sunshine.

'Well, anyhow, I've got to risk it,' muttered Jack as he slipped from the covert into the main road. 'I hope the old boy doesn't look back.' He kept on the grassy strip near the ditch, and it was well he did so, for after walking some two hundred yards, Hume suddenly stopped and looked back! Darrell had just time to throw himself flat in the ditch to avoid detection.

'Phew!' gasped the stout man, below his breath, as the old butler continued on his way, after a short survey of the road behind him. 'I hope he doesn't do that again!'

He tenderly removed a large and particularly venomous thorn from a portion of his anatomy before proceeding. Hume, however, appeared to have satisfied himself that he was not being watched, for he didn't look round again, but quickened his pace. They proceeded thus until the first straggling cottages announced the approach of the village.

Darrell allowed the old man to get well ahead, and his heart sank as he saw him turn in at a tiny chemist's shop. The owner was in the act of taking down the shutters, and wished the butler a cheerful good-morning.

Taking up his stand behind a pile of stones from whence he could command an uninterrupted view of the single street the village boasted, Jack awaited the old man's next move. It was not long in coming. The proprietor followed him into the shop, and in about three or four minutes Hume reappeared again, carrying a small white paper parcel, in addition to the one he already carried under his arm.

Was this, after all, only a shopping

expedition, thought Jack, and had he made a mistake in concluding that the parcel contained the contents of the basket? It seemed so, for on leaving the chemist's the butler went on up the busy street and paused again, this time at the post office. The chemist, however, was evidently an early riser, for the post office was not yet open. Hume turned away and commenced to retrace his steps back the way he had come. Darrell crouched down behind his screen of stones as the old man passed him.

His heart was full of chagrin, for he felt sure that he had been wasting his time. It was fairly obvious that the butler had merely been down to the village to make some purchases, possibly something for Pauline, and yet it seemed a peculiar time to choose for shopping. Of course, it might have been something that was wanted urgently at the chemist's. Then there was the brown paper parcel. The fact that Hume had stopped at the post office seemed to point to the fact that he had been going to send it off somewhere by post.

Altogether, thought Darrell disgustedly, as he commenced to follow the old man back along the road, it was a wash out!

Then, suddenly, Hume stopped, and Jack dropped again into the ditch. The old man gazed cautiously about him, and having satisfied himself that he was not observed and that as far as he knew, the road was deserted, he suddenly plunged through a gap in the hedge that ran alongside on the left and disappeared!

Darrell hauled himself laboriously out of the ditch and, keeping his eyes fixed on the point where Hume had left the road, crossed over and inspected it. It was a narrow opening caused by a small portion of the blackthorn hedge at some time having been rooted up, and beyond ran a narrow triangular shaped strip of meadow, beyond which, again, was a thick wood that led away towards the Chiltern Hills.

As he looked through the hole in the hedge, Darrell saw that the old butler was making his way across the piece of meadow land towards these woods.

'I suppose I shall only find that's a short cut to the house,' thought Jack pessimistically. 'However, here goes.'

He waited until Hume had reached the shadows of the trees, and was in the act of entering the wood before he ventured to force his way with difficulty through the gap in the hedgerow. If the old man turned now nothing could save him from discovery, but apparently Hume was quite unsuspicious, for he turned neither to left nor right, but hurried onwards in a straight line.

Darrell waited to give him time to get well within the shelter of the wood, remaining lying at full length upon the grass. After a short time had elapsed, he straightened up, and ran quickly and noiselessly over the short intervening space of turf towards the trees. He paused at the place where Hume had entered the wood, and taking cover behind the trunk of a tree, peered cautiously ahead. The figure of the old man had disappeared, but Jack could hear the faint sound of his footsteps from somewhere in front.

Dodging swiftly from tree trunk to tree trunk, Darrell hurried noiselessly in pursuit of his quarry, and presently, when the wood thinned into a little clearing, once more came in sight of the old man. He was proceeding steadily onwards, following a narrow overgrown path that twisted its way in and out among the trees.

Of one thing Darrell soon became convinced — this was certainly not a short cut to Langley Towers, for Hume was now travelling in almost the opposite direction. As this fact became evident, the stout man's spirits rose, and he began to feel that after all possibly he had not been wasting his time.

Deeper into the heart of the wooded hillside went the old butler, with Jack Darrell close at his heels. The little pathway was now so overgrown with branches and bracken that it was almost indistinguishable, and Hume seemed to find great difficulty in forcing his way among the thick tendrils. Evidently it was seldom or never used.

For nearly a mile and a half they continued thus, and then suddenly the old man left the path and turned off sharply to the right through a dense thicket. Darrell waited for a moment or two before he, too, cautiously followed. Then he drew in his breath with a sharp hiss, and his round eyes sparkled with excitement.

Before him, almost hidden by the bushes and trees, which had evidently grown up around it, stood a small, rough, wooden hut! It was so old and ramshackle that it was almost falling down. Before the rotting door Hume had stopped, and was in the act of knocking!

Jack Darrell almost stopped breathing in his excitement, as he lay among the bracken, not ten yards away, his keen eyes fixed on the scene before him.

What discovery was he about to make? Was this the hiding place of Sir Owen Langley, or did it conceal the identity of the mysterious unknown who had tried to kidnap Pauline?

Twice the old man knocked, and the second time the door was opened from within about two inches, Hume said something in a low voice, too low for Darrell to catch the words, and the door opened wider, and the butler entered, the door closing instantly behind him.

Jack determined at all costs to get a glimpse of the occupant of the hut, and with this object in view commenced to wriggle slowly forward on his stomach.

Anyone who has tried to pass through bracken interlaced with twining tendrils of briars and vine, without making a noise, will understand the difficulties of Darrell's task. His stout body had been well trained, however, in the difficult art of woodcraft by his constant association with Vyne, who, even in their school days, had always been trailing an imaginary foe and although his progress was necessarily slow, he managed to accomplish it without a sound.

He had almost reached the hut when the door suddenly opened again, and the figure of the old man reappeared. Darrell noticed that he had left behind him the larger parcel, which he guessed contained the contents of the basket he had seen the butler packing. Hume paused at the door, and said something to the hut's mysterious occupant. He was still speaking in a very low voice, almost a whisper, and Jack only managed to catch the last few words — 'If possible again tomorrow.'

A deeper voice answered from within — 'All right' — and then the door was closed and the old man turned away. He paused so close to Darrell that the stout man could almost have touched him. His eyes were curiously wet and on his face was a look of unutterable sorrow!

Jack allowed nearly five minutes to elapse after Hume's departure before he moved, then cautiously he worked his way close up to the side of the hut.

He heard the sound of the chink of glass against glass, and searching over the surface of the rotting boards he presently found what he had been seeking — a knot hole in one of the dirty planks. He applied his eyes to the hole and surveyed the interior. The hut was illuminated, for there was no window, by a single candle which was stuck on the top of a large tree stump. Seated on the floor by this and engaged in filling a glass with some wine from a bottle, was a disreputable, dirty and unshaven tramp!

7

Danger

Pauline Langley got up and bathed and dressed leisurely. The shock of the previous night had left her a little shaky and with a slight headache. Even now with the morning sunlight streaming in through her bedroom window, she could still recapture some of the horror of the night; could still see that horrible misshaped Thing with its white mask of a face bending over the bed. In her imagination she could still smell the sickly scent of the drug in her nostrils as she had smelt it when the Thing had tried to force the pad over her nose and mouth.

Who could it have been and why had she been selected for attack? What did this beastly obscene thing that came out of the night want of her? She could find no answer to either question. Something that she knew nothing about was going on around and in the vicinity of Langley Towers. Something that involved her father, and had resulted in the death of Travis, the gamekeeper, but what it was she could not conjecture.

She was far too normal and healthy to believe in the village gossip of a ghost, and anyway the thing that had come in through her window had been anything but ghostly. There was a bruise on her wrist where it had struck at her when she had struggled that testified to its tangibility.

The most probable explanation was that someone was impersonating the alleged ghost of Langley Towers for their own purpose. But who it could be or for what purpose was beyond her. The explanation that it might have some connection with the treasure she rather discounted. She had never shared the enthusiasm of her father, believing that if there had ever been any truth in the story of the hidden gold it had long since been found by some ancient Langley and spent. She had been rather surprised that Anthony Vyne should have set any store on the legend.

She finished dressing and came down

to find the house deserted. There was no sign of anybody anywhere as she wandered from room to room. Rather puzzled she went out on to the terrace and looked across the lawn. There was nobody here either. She had half expected to see Anthony and Darrell, but there was nobody in sight. Coming back through the drawing room she encountered Jennie, the parlour maid, and put a question to the girl.

'Mr. Vyne left in the car early, Miss,' said the servant. 'And Mr. Darrell went out. Mr. Cunningham's been, but Mrs. Wakefield didn't disturb you because you were sleeping. Mr. Cunningham is coming back this afternoon.'

'Thank you, Jennie,' said Pauline, and as the girl was turning away: 'Ask Hume to come and see me, will you?'

'Mr. Hume is out, too, Miss,' replied Jennie.

'Well, ask him to come to me as soon as he comes in,' said Pauline, and went back to the terrace.

Everyone apparently had gone out. She descended the steps on to the lawn and strolled aimlessly about the garden. She would have liked someone to talk to, for she felt bored and a little dispirited. Where had they all gone to?

Hume, in all probability, had gone on some errand connected with the house, but the other two? Jennie had said that Anthony had gone in the car and that Darrell had gone out, so apparently they hadn't gone together. She rather wished that Mrs. Wakefield had wakened her when Frank Cunningham had called. She would have got him to stop to lunch and keep her company. She explored the rose garden and stopped to talk to old Edwards, who was syringing the trees.

After a rambling dissertation on the habits of green fly he looked at her hesitantly and said:

'I suppose there ain't no news of Sir H'Owen, Miss?'

She shook her head.

'Not at present, Edwards,' she replied.

'An' I reckon there won't be, present or future neither,' said the old man darkly. 'An' awl the perlice an' people won't be no use, neither,' he wagged his grizzled head, sorrowfully.

In spite of the anxiety, Pauline's lips twitched.

'Why do you say that?' she asked.

'The perlice are only 'uman beings same as you and me,' said old Edwards. 'An' there's things that 'uman beings can't deal with.' He looked at her queerly. 'I reckon Sir H'Owen tried to interfere with something that weren't 'uman, an' so did poor Travis.'

'Nonsense,' said the girl half amused and half angry. 'Travis was shot. Ghosts don't use revolvers.'

'They use whatever 'appens to be 'andy, Miss,' said the old man. 'Oh yes, I knows Travis were shot an' I knows that most people 'ud laugh at me because of what I thinks. But I've 'eard things and seen things round 'ere that wants a lot of explainin'.'

'What things?' Pauline was interested. Supposing old Edwards had seen something — something that might help in unravelling the tangle.

The gardener wiped his forehead on the back of his hand and hitched up his trousers.

'What are these 'ere lights in the wood back there at nights — ' he jerked an earth-stained thumb behind his right shoulder — 'Lots o' people 'ave seen 'em. They was telling me at the Prodigal's Return only t'uther evening that Garge and Emily what's gettin' married at Christmas was walkin' through the wood night afore last and they seed 'em.'

'What sort of lights?' asked the girl.

The old man lowered his voice.

'Just a flicker o' flame deep in the 'eart o' the woods,' he said mysteriously.

Pauline smiled.

'I should think it was most likely someone lighting his pipe or cigarette,' she said practically.

'Nobody don't go through that wood after dark,' said the gardener obstinately. 'It don't lead nowhere.'

'Well, George and Emily were there,' said the girl. 'So why shouldn't there have been somebody else?'

'It's different with Garge and Emily,' said the old man. 'They be courtin'. But nobody with any sense goes there.'

This time Pauline laughed outright.

'That's hardly complimentary to George and Emily,' she said.

'Maybe it is and maybe it ain't,' replied old Edwards. 'But there yer are. Them lights don't bode no good to anyone in my opinion. I'm thankful I ain't seen 'em.'

'I think it's all very ridiculous,' said Pauline. 'What harm could they do anyone?'

'Ain't yer ever 'eard of corpse candles?' asked the gardener. 'That's wot I thinks they are. Corpse candles and they mean death!'

There was something so earnest about the old man as he said this that Pauline felt a momentary cold shiver trickle down her back.

'Surely you don't believe all that nonsense?' she said.

The gardener shook his head sadly.

'You can call it nonsense, Miss,' he replied. 'But I 'as my own ideas an' I sticks to 'em.'

'You said just now that you'd seen something,' said the girl. 'But you've only told me what you've heard. What have you seen?'

Old Edwards looked at her deliberately, glanced behind him though what he expected to see no one but himself knew.

'I've seen something around 'ere,' he said slowly, 'that I wouldn't like ter see again. No, not for all the money in the world. It lurks about in that there wood, it do.' Again he jerked his thumb over his shoulder. 'Last night I seed it just as I were goin' 'ome. It was nigh on dark afore I left off douching these roses and it were nearly dark when I seed it.'

'Seed what?' demanded Pauline in her excitement copying old Edwards' way of talking.

'Ah,' answered the old man. 'I wouldn't like ter tell yer what it were, and I didn't look too closely, I can tell yer. But it were dressed all in black and crouched — like — like a monkey.'

Pauline felt her pulses thrilling. This was a fair description of the Thing she had seen bending over her father on the lawn — the thing that had got in at her window. Old Edwards was not romancing as she had at first believed. He really had seen something.

'I think you ought to tell the police about what you saw,' she said.

The gardener sniffed contemptuously.

'The perlice,' he said disparagingly. 'What good could they do? They can only deal with flesh and blood — '

He stopped and looked round as Jennie appeared at the entrance to the rose garden.

'If you please, Miss,' said the maid. 'Mr. Cunningham's on the telephone and asking for you.'

Pauline bade the old gardener a hurried good-bye and followed Jennie back to the house.

The telephone was in the hall and the receiver stood off its hook on the table beside it. Pauline picked it up and put it to her ear. 'Is that you, Frank?' she called.

A voice, husky with suppressed excitement, answered her.

'Yes. I say, can you come over to my place at once?' it asked.

'Yes, but why? What is it?' said the girl.

'I've found your father,' came the reply, and then as she uttered an exclamation of surprise: 'But don't breathe a word to anybody. We've got to keep him lying low. He did shoot Travis.'

Pauline almost dropped the receiver in her agitation.

'But why — ' she began, when the voice over the wire stopped her.

'Don't talk any more on the 'phone,' it said. 'Come over and see me. I've got your father here now and he'll explain everything. Hurry — take the short cut through the wood.'

'All right, I'll come at once,' she replied and slammed the black cylinder back on its hook.

She waited to put on neither hat nor coat, but just as she was, flew out into the garden once more. There was a little gate at the end of a narrow path off the drive that opened into a lane and swiftly she hurried towards this.

Her brain was in a whirl. Frank had found her father and it was he who had killed the gamekeeper.

She opened the gate with trembling fingers, slipped through and closed it behind her. Two hundred yards farther along, the lane terminated in the dense wood that hemmed in Langley Towers on two sides. Through this ran a winding path that ended in meadows, and beyond that the back of Frank Cunningham's house.

Pauline almost ran along the path, avoiding the straggling roots of the thickly growing trees by instinct, for her mind was far too occupied to look where she was going.

She had reached the centre of the wood when she became aware of something moving by the path behind a screen of bushes, and then, as she drew level, a figure stepped out and caught her arm — a figure crouching and monstrous with a white patch where the face should have been.

She screamed and a hand was roughly thrust over her mouth, choking the sound back. A voice, high and squeaky, hissed in her ear.

'You have come well, my dear,' it said with a chuckle. 'And you can take it from me you'll never return!'

8

Suspense

Jack Darrell watched eagerly through the hole in the side of the shed. The tramp gulped down the wine and then turned his attention to the contents of the parcel that the old butler had brought. Some bread, half a chicken, butter and cheese. He began to eat, viciously and wolfishly, like a man who was very hungry.

Darrell frowned and thought rapidly. What should he do? Go straight away and inform the police or wait until after he had seen Anthony Vyne and acquaint him with this surprising development?

He decided rapidly that the latter would be his best course. If he informed the police he might be precipitating a scandal, for he had no idea who this unknown man might be. The butler had said that he would try and come again on the morrow, so it looked as if the tramp was likely to remain there at least until then.

Having made up his mind Darrell began to worm his way back away from the hut. Noiselessly he squirmed through the undergrowth until he judged he was far enough away to risk getting to his feet. This he did, hot and panting from his exertions, and began to walk back the way he had come. He had plenty to occupy his mind on the journey.

This fresh development had done nothing to clear up the mystery. In fact, it had, if anything, made it worse. The person he had expected to see in the hut had been Sir Owen, not this grimy and disreputable tramp. Who was he and what the deuce was Hume doing supplying him with food?

He found no explanation to satisfy him and in consequence reached Langley Towers in rather an irritable mood. He wished that Anthony had not gone dashing off to London. He wanted to discuss this surprising discovery with him. It was maddening to think that he had practically the whole day to get through before he could unburden himself to anyone. He had taken his time walking back to the house and almost the first person he saw as he mounted the steps to the terrace was Hume. The old man greeted him with a smile.

'Been for a walk, sir?' he said pleasantly. 'There's some very nice walks these parts. Some of the prettiest country in England.'

Darrell nodded.

'Yes, just been stretching my legs,' he replied. 'Where is Miss Langley?'

'I think she's out, sir,' said Hume.

Darrell's face clouded. What had Anthony said — that the girl wasn't to leave the house? Oh, that had been after dark. Well, perhaps it was all right in the daylight.

'Did she say where she was going?' he asked.

Hume shook his head.

'No, sir,' he answered. 'As a matter of fact, I didn't see her go, sir, but Jennie, the housemaid, says she had a telephone message from Mr. Cunningham so, I expect, sir, she's gone over to see him.'

Darrell's brow cleared.

That was all right if she was with Cunningham. He made himself comfortable on the terrace and read a book. Presently the heat and the fact that he had had little sleep on the night before made him feel drowsy and he dropped into a doze.

He was awakened by hearing a voice say with a chuckle: 'Well, well, that's a good way to spend a fine morning.'

He sat up and blinked at the owner of the voice. Frank Cunningham was standing grinning down at him.

'Hello,' said Darrell, yawning and struggling out of his chair. 'What are you doing here?'

'I hope,' replied Frank Cunningham, 'that I'm going to be asked to lunch. How is Miss Langley?'

Darrell stared at him.

'She's all right,' he said. 'Why, haven't you seen her?'

Cunningham shook his head.

'No,' he answered, 'she was asleep when I called this morning and they wouldn't wake her — '

'I don't mean this morning,' exclaimed the stout man, 'I mean when you telephoned — '

'Telephoned!' broke in the other. 'I haven't telephoned. What are you talking about?'

The healthy colour drained away from Darrell's face.

'You haven't telephoned!' he repeated. 'But Hume told me — just now — that Miss Langley went out after receiving a telephone message from you — '

'I never 'phoned,' said Cunningham and there was a sudden note of alarm in his voice. 'Call Hume.'

They called Hume, but the butler could give them very little information.

'It was Jennie who took the message, sir,' he said.

They sent for Jennie and she came, smiling.

'Oh, yes, Mr. Cunningham. I answered the telephone,' she said. 'Miss Langley was in the rose garden talking to Edwards and I went and fetched her — '

'Good God! But I keep telling you I never 'phoned,' cried Frank Cunningham, his face drawn and haggard.

'Well, it sounded like your voice, sir,' asserted Jennie, 'and besides you told me to tell Miss Langley that it was you speakin'.'

'But — ' began Frank and stopped as he caught a warning look from Darrell.

They got rid of Jennie and the butler and when they had gone, Darrell turned to the other.

'Look here,' he said gravely, 'I didn't want to say anything in front of those two, but this looks very serious to me.'

'It does to me,' said Frank hoarsely. 'I certainly never telephoned, so whoever did and used my name must have done so to get Pauline out of the house.'

'That's exactly what I think,' agreed Darrell, 'and I'm damned scared.'

Frank's face went even paler.

'Good God! You don't think — ' he began.

'After last night, I'm willing to think anything,' snapped Darrell rapidly. 'I wish to God Anthony was here, but as he isn't we must do what we can ourselves. Listen! That message was sent to decoy Miss

Langley out of the house. Therefore, it must have asked her to meet you somewhere. Supposing it had really been you and you wanted to see her, what would you have said?'

'I should either have suggested coming over here,' said Frank, 'or asked her to come and see me.'

'Exactly,' Darrell nodded quickly. 'Now if she was going to see you which way would she have gone?'

'The quickest way is through the wood — Where the devil are you going to?' Frank broke off as Darrell, moving with surprising speed for a man of his bulk, began to descend the steps of the terrace.

'Through the wood!' answered the fat man over his shoulder. 'To see if we can pick up any traces of her. We've got to do something and that's the only thing I can think of.'

Springing down the steps, Cunningham joined him and they raced side by side towards the little gate through which Pauline had passed earlier. It was dark and forbidding under cover of the trees, and filled with a vague foreboding they sped along the twisting path in silence. Each was conscious of a secret dread as to what they might find that they were reluctant to put into words. They had reached the centre of the wood when Darrell, whose eyes were scanning the ground, saw something glitter, and stopped dead.

'What is it?' panted Frank as the other pulled up quickly.

For answer the stout man stooped and picked up the little object that had caught his eye. It was a small diamond bar brooch.

'That's Pauline's,' cried Cunningham instantly as he glanced at it.

Darrell said nothing but peered at the ground where the brooch had been lying. Several dark patches showed up on the soil of the path and, stooping he applied his finger to one of them. When he straightened up and looked at the tip it was wet with fresh blood!

9

Found!

Pauline heard the words uttered by the horrible creature who held her and shuddered, but she did not lose her presence of mind. Her brain was working at express speed to find some means of escape from her assailant, and suddenly a plan suggested itself. With a little shuddering sob she allowed herself to go quite limp and closed her eyes.

She heard him utter an exclamation and the arms that held her tightened their hold. His hot breath fanned her face as he bent down to look closer at her.

'Fainted, eh?' he muttered. 'Well, it'll save a lot of trouble.'

He shifted his clasp in order to pick her up bodily, and suddenly exerting all her strength, she twisted free of his encircling arms.

He ripped out a startled oath and made

a grab at her as she ran away, and his fingers gripped her shoulder. She twisted her head swiftly and her teeth sank into that clutching hand. She heard a grunt of pain and the grasp relaxed.

Without looking behind her she stumbled blindly into the depths of the wood, running as she had never run before. The pain in his hand, from which the blood was streaming, brought the unknown to a halt, and the momentary chance gave Pauline a start.

Pushing her way through the tangled undergrowth and praying that she wouldn't stumble she sped on. She could hear his footfalls behind her and the snapping of the branches as he forced his way through, but she was fleeter of foot than her pursuer and kept her lead.

The way got rougher, the undergrowth more dense, but she kept on. In her panic she had lost her sense of direction, and although she did not realise it she was running for help in the direction that help was least likely to be found. Once she threw a terrified glance behind her and saw that in spite of all her efforts her pursuer was gaining on her.

She redoubled her speed. Her breath was whistling through her clenched teeth and there was a dull little pain in her side. Mists of black and red swam before her eyes and the blood pounded in her head. She knew that she could not keep going for very much longer.

The wood was thinning. Once in the open she would stand little hope. Her legs felt like lead and her heart thumped madly, but blindly, desperately, she ran on, her sheer panic lent her strength above the normal.

Once more she looked back. The figure behind her was nearer now and steadily gaining. Before her was a straggling screen of tangled bushes and undergrowth. She forced her way through and then her feet trod on — nothing!

She gave a choked scream and clutched wildly at the branch of a tree, but it tore through her fingers. She felt herself falling, flung herself backwards and went sliding and slithering down a steep slope . . .

* * *

Frank Cunningham looked at the crimson tip of Darrell's finger with horror.

'Good God!' he breathed. 'What has happened here?'

The stout man shook his head.

'Only God knows,' he answered gravely and looked about him.

There were signs on the soft surface of the path of a struggle. The ground had been churned up and he could see the marks of high heeled shoes. They led away into the heart of the wood and were obliterated in places by the broad print of a heavier shoe.

He pointed them out to Cunningham and together they followed the trail until it ended abruptly among the bracken. There were, however, plenty of traces to show which way the girl had gone. The undergrowth was trampled down and the branches of the low growing bushes broken.

With hearts that were for the most part in their mouths with the fear of what they might find, they pressed forward. The trail went on and presently they found that they were coming to the end of the wood.

'Be careful here,' warned Frank Cunningham below his breath as they advanced. 'There's an almost sheer drop into an old quarry on the other side of these bushes.'

Darrell nodded and then he stopped and pointed.

'Look here,' he muttered.

Cunningham's eyes followed the direction of his outstretched arm and he saw. The trail led straight up to the screen of bushes that marked the lip of the old quarry.

'This is terrible — ' he began hoarsely, and stopped as Darrell gripped his arm.

'Listen!' whispered the stout man.

From somewhere close at hand came a faint cry and the voice was that of a woman.

Cunningham forced his way through the bushes and when Darrell joined him he was lying at full length, peering down into the pit on the other side.

The cry came again, more clearly and now they could distinguish the words: 'Help! Help!'

Looking in the direction of the sound,

Darrell saw below him the figure of a girl. She was lying crumpled up by the side of a large boulder.

Cunningham called down. 'Hello, Pauline,' he cried anxiously. 'Are you hurt?'

They saw her turn her face upwards and then a weak voice answered him.

'I — I — don't know,' it said shakily. 'I don't think so.'

'I'm coming down,' said Cunningham and began to make his way down the sloping side of the quarry.

It was difficult going, but he managed to find a foothold and eventually reached the girl's side. She was lying on a heap of sand and to this fact she owed her life. Had she fallen a yard to the left she would have struck the boulder. He knelt anxiously beside her and supported her head on his arm.

'I think it was the shock mostly,' she said. 'I remember falling and then I think I must have fainted.' She looked fearfully around. 'Have you got — him?' she asked.

Cunningham shook his head.

'We haven't got anyone,' he replied. 'What happened?'

'It was the Hunchback,' she whispered. 'He — was waiting in the wood and — ' She shivered. 'Oh, it was horrible — horrible. I've never been so frightened in my life.'

'Don't think about it,' said Frank soothingly. 'What we've got to do now, is to get you out of here and home.'

This was easier said than done, but they managed it between them. The soft sand had acted as a buffer and they discovered that beyond a few bruises the girl had suffered no serious hurt, and eventually they got her back to Langley Towers and into the tender care of Mrs. Wakefield.

Frank Cunningham stayed for the rest of the afternoon discussing the matter with Darrell and did not leave until tea time.

After that Darrell was left to himself until Anthony Vyne came back just after the dressing gong had sounded for dinner. He was tired, hot and dusty after his journey, but he listened gravely to Darrell's account of the attempt on Pauline Langley.

‘That’s twice,’ he said when his friend had finished. ‘Well, we’ve got to see to it that there’s no third time.’

10

A Pistol Shot

Darrell sat on the edge of the bed while he dressed and related his tracking of the butler to the wood and the discovery of the tramp in the hut.

The reporter listened without interruption during his friend's recital.

'It doesn't seem to help matters, does it?' concluded Darrell. 'I was expecting to find that it was Sir Owen in the hut, which would, at least, have cleared up one mystery.'

Anthony gazed thoughtfully into the mirror as he carefully brushed his hair.

'As you say, old chap,' he murmured after a pause, 'it certainly does not help us much.'

'Do you think this tramp can be the Black Hunchback?' asked Jack.

Vyne shook his head decidedly.

'No, I am sure he isn't,' he replied.

'Unless my suspicions are completely wrong, I think I can hazard a guess as to the identity of the Black Hunchback.'

'Who do you think it is then?' asked his friend eagerly.

'I'm not prepared to say at the moment,' answered Anthony. 'But I made one or two enquiries in London which I think will later tend to throw some light upon the mystery. Who this tramp can be, and for what reason Hume is supplying him with food I can't for the moment imagine. You're sure it wasn't Sir Owen?'

'Positive,' asserted Darrell. 'I've only seen photographs of Sir Owen, it's true, but this man is different in every way — shorter and much stouter.'

'Well, anyhow, there seems no fear of him moving from where he is at the moment,' said Vyne, buttoning his waistcoat. 'From what you heard the butler say on leaving, it's obvious that he intends visiting the hut again tomorrow, probably with more food, and this time we'll both be present, and force him to disclose the man's identity. In the meantime, we must do nothing to rouse Hume's suspicions, as he may warn the man and we should find the bird flown.'

They descended to the dining room, and found that Pauline had got up for dinner. The long rest had done her good and, except for a slight pallor, she seemed none the worse for her adventures.

The meal was nearing its conclusion when Anthony put a question to the girl that caused Darrell to open his eyes wide with astonishment.

'Miss Langley, are you aware if your father's first wife had any relations alive at the time of her marriage?' he enquired suddenly after a short silence.

The girl thought for a moment before replying. 'She was an orphan when daddy first met her,' she replied at length, 'but I believe she had a brother.'

'You don't know where this brother is at the present time?' asked the reporter.

Pauline shook her head.

'I don't even know whether he is still alive,' she answered. 'Daddy never spoke much about his first marriage, and naturally I never questioned him.'

'What was his first wife's maiden

name?' enquired Vyne,

'Fearon,' answered the girl. 'Mercia Fearon. Daddy met her abroad, somewhere in the Argentine, I believe — ' She broke off and looked at Anthony curiously. 'Why are you so interested, Mr. Vyne? You surely don't think that it can have any bearing on daddy's strange disappearance?'

'My experience has taught me, Miss Langley,' said the reporter, smiling, 'that it is possible to pick up a clue from all sorts of unlikely information.'

The subject dropped, the conversation drifting into other channels. Just as they had finished coffee, which was served on the terrace, Inspector Person called to inform them that the inquest on Travis would be held on the following Thursday — in two days' time.

Vyne called the Inspector aside as he was leaving.

'Do you have many tramps round this way?' he asked.

Person scratched his large head reflectively.

'Well, no, Mr. Vyne,' he answered,

slowly and ponderously, 'I can't say as 'ow we does. These parts 'as always bin pretty free of them gentry.'

'You haven't noticed a tramp lurking about the vicinity recently?' continued the reporter, 'a short man, rather stout?'

The Inspector slowly shook his head.

'Can't say I 'ave, sir,' he answered; 'But I'll make h'enquiries. Do you think that poor Travis was killed by a tramp?'

'No, no,' replied Anthony, 'I was just asking out of curiosity that's all. I thought I saw a tramp hanging about the main road as I came through the village this evening. As they are unpleasant customers to have around, I thought I'd just mention it. I must have been mistaken.'

'Anyhow, I'll keep a look h'out,' said Inspector Person, 'and if there is I'll soon shift him — we don't want 'em round 'ere.'

The Inspector took his departure, and shortly afterwards, leaving Darrell to entertain the girl, Anthony walked slowly down to the post office. He kept a sharp look out, as he strolled along, mindful of his previous experience, but nothing occurred, and having sent off a long telegram to the editor of *The Messenger*, he proceeded to enjoy a quiet walk in the gathering dusk of the beautiful summer evening.

As he sauntered slowly along, his pipe between his teeth, he sorted and resorted in his mind all the facts of the case as he knew them.

Sir Owen Langley had been interested in the legend of the treasure of Langley Towers and, according to Pauline, had discovered the hidden meaning of the doggerel verse which had been left behind by his ancestor, Sir Hugo Lang, as a clue to the hiding place of the bullion. Immediately on the top of this knowledge, Sir Owen had very mysteriously disappeared, rushing out of the house in the middle of the night in his pyjamas and dressing gown and vanishing apparently into thin air! Also round about this time had appeared on the scene the figure of the Black Hunchback which had been seen first by Travis lurking round Langley Towers three nights before his death, and secondly by Pauline on the night of her father's disappearance and the gamekeeper's murder.

Surely there must be some connecting link between all these happenings. Following this had occurred the shot at himself, as he was walking back after leaving Frank Cunningham, and the twice attempted abduction of Pauline Langley. The finding of the revolver and the little gold ball seemed to point conclusively to the fact that Sir Owen was guilty of the murder of Travis, and yet Anthony could not bring himself to believe in this possibility.

True, it accounted for his strange and inexplicable disappearance, but the reporter refused to believe that it was the real reason.

He had formed a theory that fitted all the facts in his possession — a theory so startling that he hesitated to put it into words. It accounted for every incident that had occurred, save one. And that was what was bothering Anthony Vyne at the moment.

In no possible way could he fit into his solution of the puzzle the discovery of the tramp in the hut in the wood. As he walked slowly along the quiet and peaceful country road he tried vainly to account for the presence of this new factor in the case.

Who was the occupant of the hut, and why should Hume bother to supply him with food? Could it be possible that his theory was after all the wrong one, and that the tramp was Sir Owen, after all? Certainly Darrell had said that there was no resemblance, but then he had only seen photographs of Sir Owen, and it would have been quite easy for him to have been mistaken particularly if Sir Owen had disguised himself.

If such were the case it tended rather to confirm Darrell and Frank Cunningham's idea that Sir Owen was responsible for the death of the gamekeeper, and was at the bottom of the other strange happenings round Langley Towers. But Vyne couldn't bring himself to believe that Sir Owen was in any way accountable for the attempt on Pauline. It was unthinkable that a man should try to abduct his own daughter, and besides, what possible motive could he have for doing so?

No, there must be some other explanation to account for the presence of the tramp. Could he possibly be the mysterious unknown who was masquerading as the Black Hunchback?

That was a great deal more like it, and but for the fact that it was Hume who was supplying him with food, Anthony could have believed that possible. But then it meant that the old butler was in the plot against Pauline and Sir Owen, and Anthony, who was an excellent judge of character, felt certain that the old man was deeply devoted to the girl and to his master, and was the last person likely to be a party to anything that was going to cause them harm.

His thoughts swung back to his first theory, and for the hundredth time he stringently analysed it, viewing it from every possible angle.

Lost in thought the reporter failed to notice a ragged unshaven figure peer at him as he passed from between the closely growing trunks of two trees in the wood that edged the road. The tramp watched the tall athletic form as it swung along, until it was lost to view in the gathering darkness, and then turned and slunk back into the gloomy depths of the wood. Every now and again, as he proceeded, his upper lip curled back in a snarl curiously reminiscent of a wolf, revealing yellow, broken teeth.

Suddenly he stopped dead and listened intently, his body bent forward slightly. It was quite dark now, and in the stillness of the new-born night, the slightest sound travelled for a long distance. It was only a breaking twig that had caused him to stop, but into the bloodshot eyes of the tramp sprang an expression of fear.

Again came the sharp snap-snap, and the tramp crouched down behind a tree trunk concealing himself among the thick undergrowth.

The moon had not yet risen, and the wood was almost pitch dark. The faint snapping of the twigs came nearer, then ceased altogether. Then came the sound of the scraping of a match and almost at once a little yellow flame broke the darkness. It revealed to the eyes of the tramp the figure of a man.

The newcomer held the match he had struck to a watch on his wrist. For a second only it flared up before he blew it out, but in that second the light had fallen full upon his face.

The tramp gave a violent start, and it took all his will to suppress the startled cry that rose to his lips. The man who had lighted the match moved off in total ignorance of the fact that behind him, silently and shadow-like, followed the figure of the tramp.

Anthony turned into the drive leading up to Langley Towers, his mind still deeply engrossed with the problem he was setting his brain to solve, but he arrived at the house long before he had come to any conclusion which satisfied him.

Making his way to the drawing room, he discovered Darrell and Pauline engaged in a conversation concerning the relative merits of two well-known film stars.

'Hello!' said the stout man, looking up as Anthony entered. 'I was just beginning to wonder where you'd got to.'

'I've been down to the village to send a wire,' answered the reporter.

'One of the servants would have taken it, Mr. Vyne,' said the girl.

'If confession is good for the soul,' answered Anthony, smiling, 'exercise is good for the liver. I hope Jack had not been boring you with his views on the silent drama. Unless checked at the outset he is apt to become somewhat wordy — between meals.'

Darrell snorted. 'Well, I like that,' he cried indignantly. 'I — '

'I think he has been most amusing,' interposed Pauline smiling.

'Oh, he usually is,' agreed Vyne, crossing to the fireplace, and dropping into a chair. 'In fact — '

He broke off sharply. The French windows leading on to the terrace were wide open, and suddenly from outside close at hand, came the staccato sound of a pistol shot!

Vyne was on his feet in an instant.

'Come on, Jack! Stay where you are, Miss Langley,' he shouted, and made a dash for the open window.

'Where do you think it came from?' cried Darrell as he panted after his friend.

'I'm not sure — quite close though,' said Anthony, racing down the steps of the terrace on to the lawn.

'Somewhere near the rose garden, I should say,' gasped Darrell, keeping up with his friend's long strides.

They crossed the stretch of grass at a run. On reaching the steps leading down to the rose garden Vyne paused and sniffed the still air.

In spite of the perfume of the roses a strong acrid smell was wafted to their nostrils — the scent of cordite.

'The shot was fired close here,' said Anthony. 'You can still — '

'Look! Over there by the door leading to the Home Covert!' cried Darrell excitedly.

The yellow disc of the moon was just rising and already her light was strong enough to turn the darkness into a faint grey. Anthony's eyes followed the direction of his friend's pointing finger.

A dark object lay outstretched upon the path by the door. Without a word Vyne hurried over, with Darrell close at his heels. It was the still figure of a man.

Stooping, the reporter turned the body over gently, and felt for the heart.

'Quite dead,' he said tonelessly, a moment later. 'The vicinity of the Home Covert appears to be a particularly dangerous neighbourhood. I wonder who this poor fellow is.'

He felt in his pocket; produced a box of matches, and struck a light. As the light shone full upon the face of the dead man on the ground, Darrell gave a cry of astonishment and started back.

It was the body of the tramp he had seen in the hut that morning, and he had been shot through the head!

11

The Black Hunchback

The sound of voices came to them from the direction of the house and Vyne gripped Darrell's arm as he recognised one of the voices as belonging to the old butler — Hume.

'Quick, old man,' he whispered swiftly. 'Slip up and tell Hume to 'phone for a doctor and the police, but don't tell him who it is that has been shot. Go quickly and bring my torch back with you.'

Left alone, Anthony stood for several seconds gazing thoughtfully at the body of the tramp, his fingers caressing his chin. Then he went over to the door in the wall that separated the rose garden from the covert beyond, and pressed against it gently. It was locked! Vyne pursed his lips. Evidently the tramp had not entered that way. What had he been doing in the rose garden at all? It was a question, to which the reporter could find no answer.

In a short while Darrell returned with the torch,

'Inspector Person and the doctor are on their way, old man,' he announced as he handed his friend the electric torch.

'We've got ten minutes or so to ourselves,' muttered Anthony, flashing a bright white circle of light on the body of the tramp. 'Hold this a minute, Jack,' he said crisply, handing his companion back the torch and dropping upon his knees beside the dead man.

Deftly and swiftly his hands flashed over the man's ragged clothes, but beyond a half-empty packet of Gold Flake cigarettes and a box of matches, he found nothing.

'Not much there,' he muttered, replacing the things which he had found there, and rising to his feet. 'Come over to the wall and shine the light along near the top.'

Halfway along the wall to the right of the door, Anthony stopped.

'This is where he got over,' he said, pointing to several deep scratches in the lichen with which the wall was covered.

'Look, this piece of moss has been torn away.' He picked up a little tuft of moss from the narrow bed below the wall.

'Give me the light a minute,' he said sharply as he stooped. Darrell gave him the torch, and Vyne directed its beam on the soft earth of the flower bed. The stout man bent forward eagerly as the light revealed a jumbled set of footprints in the mould.

Anthony looked at them for some seconds before he spoke.

'Humph!' he muttered almost to himself. 'The murderer got over first, followed by the tramp.

'How do you know that?' asked Darrell curiously.

'If you look at the tramp's boots,' answered Vyne, 'you will see that he is wearing a pair of square-toed ones, obviously nearly new. Now here, in nearly every case, the square-toed boots over-trod and obliterated the prints made by the murderer's boots, which are longer and narrower. Obviously, therefore, the murderer got over the wall first, followed by the tramp. How long after it is, of course, impossible to say.'

'But what was the tramp doing in the rose garden?' asked Darrell.

'That's just what I'm wondering,' said Vyne. 'Of course, if the murderer is our friend of last night, there's not much doubt as to what he was doing, but I can't account for the presence of the tramp in the case at all.'

'Perhaps he was following the Black Hunchback,' suggested his friend.

'I shouldn't be surprised if you're not right, although I can't see what his object could have been,' agreed Vyne. 'Don't say any more now,' he added quickly. 'I think I can hear our friend, Inspector Person, approaching.'

He proved to be right, for a moment later the short, fat figure of the Inspector accompanied by another man, appeared at the top of the steps leading down to the rose garden.

'This is h'a terrible business, h'a terrible business,' said Person, as he came up to Vyne. 'Another murder almost with'hin a 'undred yards of the h'other. Who is the man, Mr. Vyne? Have you h'any idea?'

The reporter shook his head.

'I haven't the faintest idea, Inspector,' he replied. 'He looks to me like a tramp.'

'A tramp, eh?' exclaimed Person. 'That's funny! You were asking me about tramps h'earlier in the h'evening.'

Anthony made no reply, and the doctor proceeded to make a cursory examination by the light of a torch.

'Death must have been instantaneous,' he announced a short while later. 'He was stone dead almost before he reached the ground. The bullet entered the left temple, passed through the brain, and came out just by the base of the skull.'

'Anything to h'identify the man h'on the body?' asked the Inspector.

'I've been through his pockets, but there was nothing on him at all,' said Anthony, 'except a half-empty packet of cigarettes and a box of matches.'

'Humph!' said the Inspector, scratching his head, a habit which appeared to be a favourite one with him. 'That don't 'elp us much. I wonder what 'e was doin' in 'ere. Looking for a chance to break in, I suppose.'

'It seems to be rather an unfortunate

place round here,' interposed the doctor, as he straightened up. 'First, poor Travis, and now this chap. Well, I don't think I can be of any further service, Inspector. I'll drop my report in to the station later. Good night, gentlemen.'

As he was moving away, the Inspector called after him. 'H'if you're going past the station, doctor,' he said, 'you might ask 'em to send h'up the h'ambulance.'

'All right, I will,' replied the doctor, looking back from the top of the steps, and the next minute he was gone in the shadow of the shrubbery.

'Well, Mr. Vyne,' said Person, when they were alone, 'what do you make of h'it h'all?'

'At the moment, I can make nothing of it,' declared Anthony candidly.

'It seems as though we was having a regular h'epidemic of murders round 'ere lately, don't it?' continued Person, shaking his massive head. 'I don't mind telling you that there are h'all sorts o' strange rumours goin' about the village.'

'Oh,' said the reporter, with sudden interest, 'what sort of rumours?'

'Well, for one thing,' replied the Inspector, 'they say as 'ow the ghost o' Langley Towers 'as appeared agin. Several people 'ave seen it. An' Travis is supposed to 'ave seen it three nights afore 'e was killed. I can tell you, sir, there's a regular scare in the village, and not one of 'em 'ud come around 'ere after dark not for a 'undred quid, they wouldn't.'

'Evidently,' thought Vyne, 'old Edwards, the gardener, has been talking.'

'And there's h'another thing,' Person went on. 'It's got around that something has happened to Sir Owen.'

'It is a mistake to believe all you hear, Inspector,' murmured Anthony. 'Sir Owen is certainly away at the moment, but I've no doubt that it will not be very long before he is back again.'

'Oh, I'm not saying that I believe h'in all these rumours myself,' said Person hastily, 'but you know what gossip h'is in a little neighbourhood like this 'ere. If you'll wait 'ere a minute; sir, I think I'll just slip h'up to the 'ouse and telephone to the station to make sure about the h'ambulance.'

'All right, Inspector,' said Anthony, and Person hurried away.

'It seems that Sir Owen's disappearance is beginning to get talked about,' remarked Darrell, as soon as he was out of earshot.

'It was bound to happen, old man,' replied Vyne. 'You can't stop servants from gossiping. It is a wonder to me that it hasn't leaked out before.'

He relapsed into silence and Darrell refrained from any further remark, for he knew that his friend was engaged in puzzling over the mysterious death of the tramp and trying to connect it with the rest of the problem.

Anthony was, as a matter of fact, deeply perplexed. Who was this tramp, and why should he have been murdered? He was certainly not disguised in any way. The reporter had made sure of that during his brief examination of the body. His thoughts were interrupted by the sound of a hurried footfall over the lawn.

He glanced sharply at the entrance to the rose garden, as the agitated figure of old Hume, the butler, loomed in view.

The old man was greatly excited, and his voice sounded curiously husky as he spoke. Is — is that you, Mr. Vyne?' he asked. 'Inspector Person has just told me that it's a — a tramp who has been shot. Is that true?'

He had come to a halt in front of the reporter, and Anthony could see even in the pale light of the moon that his face was white and drawn, and that his hands were tightly clenched as though he was passing through an intense emotional strain.

'It's quite true, Hume,' he answered quietly.

'Could I — ' Hume hesitated and seemed to have great difficulty in articulating his words; 'could I see the — the body?'

With a feeling that he was on the verge of making a momentous discovery, Anthony led the way over to the dead man without another word, shining the light of his torch full upon the upturned face.

The old man drew near, trembling in every limb. He looked down, and the next instant with a great cry had fallen on his knees beside the body, his arms outstretched over the silent figure.

'Oh, God!' he moaned, between broken sobs that shook his frame like a branch in a high wind. 'Jim! Jim! Jim!'

Anthony stooped and laid his hand kindly on the old man's heaving shoulders.

'Come, come, Hume,' he said; 'you must pull yourself together. Do you know the man?'

The butler looked up at him dumbly, and Anthony saw that tears were streaming down the lined old face, but he did not answer the reporter's question.

Vyne waited a little while to give him time to recover himself before speaking again, then:

'I think it would be better if you were to be quite candid with me, Hume,' he said gently. 'Who is this man?'

The old man's lips moved, but it was some time before the words he was trying to utter made themselves audible.

'He was my son!' he managed to jerk out at last.

To say that Anthony and Darrell were surprised would be to put it too mildly. The reporter had been expecting a revelation, but nothing like the true one. So this was the solution of the mystery surrounding the tramp. This piece of human jetsam was the old butler's son.

'What was he doing here, and why was he hiding in the hut in the wood?' asked Anthony as soon as he had recovered from his astonishment.

Hume had managed by an obvious effort to partially control his emotion.

'I don't know what he was doing here, Mr. Vyne,' he replied shakily, 'but I can tell you why he was hiding in the hut. It can't make any difference now.' He rose unsteadily to his feet, and Darrell slipped an arm supportively through his.

'Have you ever heard of 'Soapy' Davis?' asked Hume tremulously, after a slight pause.

Vyne started.

'You mean the safe-breaker?' he enquired quickly. 'Got his nickname from his habit of taking impressions of office and hotel keys on cakes of soap.'

Hume nodded his white head.

'That was poor Jim,' he said sadly. 'I suppose it will all come out at the inquest?'

'But I thought that Davis was in prison,' said the reporter.

The old man let his eyes rest for a moment on the still form at his feet, then he turned them back to Vyne.

'He was, Mr. Vyne,' he said, almost in a whisper. 'But he managed to break prison a week ago and made his way to me. He knew that I was in service with Sir Owen. I'm afraid he's a bit wild, but he wasn't all bad. You see, sir, his mother died when he was quite a little chap, and he got mixed up with the wrong set; got in first with one of the racing gangs, and that was the start of it.

'I lost sight of him for several years, and I didn't know where he was or what had become of him until I received a letter from him from the prison. Then when he turned up here one night, almost dead from hunger and fatigue, I did my best to help him . . . I knew no one ever went near the old charcoal burner's hut in

Colethorpe Woods, and I thought he could lie low there perhaps until after the hue and cry had died down.

'He promised me that if he could get away abroad, he'd turn over a new leaf. You see, Mr. Vyne, whatever he was, I always saw him as I remember him best . . . a little chap . . . ' Hume's voice broke, and he choked back a little sob. 'You can't very well blame me, can you, sir?' he asked, almost pleadingly.

Anthony laid a hand gently on the old man's broad shoulders.

'No, Hume, I don't blame you at all,' he said, a note of sympathy in his voice. 'I suppose, under the circumstances, I should have behaved in the same way myself. Tell me, does anyone else know about this, besides you and I?'

'No, sir,' answered Hume. 'I always let it be supposed that Jim had died abroad.'

'Then if you take my advice,' said the reporter, 'I should leave it at that. It will save you a lot of unnecessary trouble, and the truth in this case can do no one any good. I suppose, technically, I am compounding a felony, but under the circumstances I feel that I am justified.'

Hume looked gratefully at him.

'Thank you, sir,' he said simply. 'I see that what you say is right.'

'There's one thing, Hume, I should like to ask you,' said Anthony after a pause. 'Is there any reason that you know about, for his having been shot?'

Hume shook his head.

'None,' he answered, 'unless it was the same person as shot poor Travis.'

'Of course the reason for his being in the rose garden is cleared up,' put in Darrell; 'he was probably waiting for a chance of seeing you.'

'I think you're wrong there, sir, if you'll excuse me saying so,' said the butler. 'He promised me faithfully that he wouldn't come near the house, and it was too risky for him to take a chance of being seen by anyone.'

'You're sure that he had nothing to do with the murder of Travis, or the disappearance of Sir Owen?' asked Anthony.

'Quite, sir,' answered Hume emphatically. 'Poor Jim was a bit bad, there's no denying that, but he wouldn't have killed anyone. As a matter of fact, he had a horror of firearms of all sorts ever since he was a kid.'

Vyne nodded.

'I seem to remember that Davis was never known to carry a gun,' he remarked. 'Besides I — ' He broke off quickly. 'Here comes Person again,' he whispered. 'Not a word.'

The Inspector was accompanied by two constables, carrying a light stretcher,

'H'I am sorry to 'ave been so long, Mr. Vyne,' he apologised. 'H'I 'ad some difficulty in getting through.'

They looked on in silence as the remains of the dead convict were lifted on to the stretcher. As it was being carried away, Hume made a move forward, but Anthony laid a warning hand on the old man's arm, and he stopped.

'H'I 'ope as 'ow you'll let me know h'if you discover anything, Mr. Vyne,' said Person just before he left. 'It'll mean a feather in my cap h'if I can clear h'up these two crimes.'

'I think I can give you a piece of information now,' said the reporter. 'I believe that I have been able to identify the body.'

Inspector Person rubbed his fat hands gleefully. 'Who was it?' he enquired.

'I think you'll find that he was an escaped convict known as 'Soapy' Davis.' He glanced sideways at Hume. 'I recognised him just after you had gone to 'phone.'

'That's h'a great 'elp,' said the Inspector. 'Thank you very much, Mr. Vyne.' He went off, following the two constables and their grim burden.

Anthony was in a thoughtful mood as a few minutes later he walked slowly across the lawn, with Darrell and the old butler. Halfway to the house, he stopped suddenly and turned back.

'Where are you going?' asked Darrell, as his friend started to retrace his steps.

'I shan't be long, old man,' replied Anthony. 'I just want to have a look at something.'

'Shall I come with you?' asked his friend.

'No,' exclaimed Vyne, 'you go back and keep Miss Langley company. She must be wondering what has happened, and besides I don't like the idea of leaving her alone so long now that darkness has fallen.'

He swung off and made his way to the rose garden. Arrived there, he went straight to the place where, by the marks on the wall, he had found the way by which the escaped convict and the man who had been responsible for his death had gained access to the garden. He stopped and looked up at the wall, then moved along for two or three yards to the right. With a sudden quick spring, he caught the coping with his hands, and in a trice had pulled himself up and was astride the wall. The next instant he had slipped down on the other side and found himself in the Home Covert.

Anthony stopped and brushed the dust from his clothes, then he walked slowly along until he arrived at the spot where the wall had been climbed.

Taking the torch from his pocket where he had thrust it after his investigation of the body of Davis, he directed its light upon the ground at his feet. The next moment he gave vent to a little exclamation of disappointment. He had been hoping to find some traces that might have given him a clue to the identity of the tramp's murderer, but on this side of the wall the ground was hard and stony, and yielded nothing. He swept the light of his torch round, and presently came upon a small depression under a clump of trees where the earth seemed moist.

He moved over towards it, and here he found what he had been looking for. The clearly defined impression of a long and narrow shoe!

It was the same in every detail as that on the other side of the wall. The print of the murderer's foot! A little further on Anthony came across another, but here it was partially obliterated by the mark of the square-toed boots worn by the escaped convict — Davis.

Here was clear proof that the tramp had been following the man with the narrow shoe. Vyne followed the trail of footprints slowly. As he penetrated deeper and deeper into the wood, the ground grew softer, and the prints more frequent. All at once he came to a clearing in the trees, and here the ground was hard and stony again, and he lost the trail.

He cast round in every direction, but he could find no other signs of either the square-toed boots or the narrow ones.

Suddenly he snapped off the light of his torch, and his body grew tense and rigid. A slight sound had reached his ears from the heart of the forest ahead!

Anthony slipped quickly behind the trunk of a tree and listened with straining ears. He had not been mistaken. Someone ahead was forcing their way through the undergrowth! Could it be the mysterious masquerader — the Black Hunchback!

A thrill ran through Anthony's veins at the chance of coming to close grips with the unknown. The sounds ceased suddenly as though, whoever it was, had stopped to listen. After a slight pause they recommenced.

The moon was high in the heavens by now, and at one point ahead in the wood a single ray of light penetrated the trees and shone full upon a small open space of ground beneath.

Would the marauder pass through this shaft of light? As far as the reporter could judge by the sound the unknown was travelling in that direction.

Anthony Vyne kept his eyes glued to the patch of moonlight. The seconds went slowly by, and to the waiting man they seemed to drag on leaden feet. Surely, the nocturnal prowler must have passed that moonlit space by now? Anthony had almost made up his mind that he had, when suddenly he appeared in the silvery light!

The reporter's jaw tightened, and almost unconsciously his hands clenched until the fingers bit into the palms.

A stunted, misshapen figure! The figure of a dwarf dressed in some garment that showed ebon-hued in the ray of moonlight. The Black Hunchback! Where the face should have been, was nothing but a shapeless white smudge!

Swiftly the Thing hurried along in a curiously crouched position, and the next instant had vanished in the darkness beyond the patch of light.

Instantly Anthony was off in pursuit! Quite accidentally he had stumbled on a chance of clearing up the identity of the mysterious Phantom that haunted Langley

Towers, and he determined this time he would make no mistake.

Swiftly and noiselessly, he sped in the direction taken by the figure in black. In and out among the trees he twisted, and shortly they began to thin out. In a little while they would reach open country!

Presently he came in sight of his quarry not more than a hundred yards away! At the same instant he trod suddenly upon the dry branch of a tree. It broke beneath his weight with a report like a pistol shot! The figure in front stopped, swung round and saw him! At once it was off at full speed, making for the edge of the wood, where it gave on to a stretch of meadow.

Anthony, realising that concealment was no longer possible, went running in pursuit like an arrow released from a bow.

But the man he was chasing could run, and run well. He had suddenly straightened up on seeing the reporter, and was revealed as a fairly tall man. With long easy strides he covered the ground at an incredible speed. They had reached the open meadow by now, and Anthony put on a spurt.

Slowly, inch by inch, he began to overtake his quarry, but in spite of his splendid condition the strain was beginning to tell on him. Even his well-trained muscles couldn't keep up such a terrific pace for long. Less than fifty yards separated them now, and Anthony suddenly made a supreme effort. He literally seemed to fly over the ground. And then, without warning, the figure in front suddenly stumbled and fell headlong!

Before he could rise Vyne was on him and had pinned him to the ground. Like a maniac he struggled to free himself, but with a quick twist Anthony had him helpless in a jujitsu lock.

'Now, my friend, I think I'll have a look at you,' he panted grimly.

He jerked his captive round on to his back. The man's face was concealed beneath a white silk handkerchief, and with a sudden quick pull Anthony ripped it off.

Then he started back with an exclamation of astonishment.

For he was looking full into the upturned face of Frank Cunningham!

12

The Gravel Pit!

'Good Heavens!' gasped Cunningham, 'it's Mr. Vyne!'

For some seconds Anthony was too utterly astounded to speak. It seemed incredible to believe that Cunningham was the Black Hunchback! And yet if he were to rely upon the evidence of his own eyes, it was impossible to think otherwise. If such was really the truth, then this preconceived theory was completely shattered.

'It's all right, Mr. Vyne,' continued the young man, panting. 'You can let me go! If I'd known that it was you, I wouldn't have run away. I thought it was the other fellow.'

'What other fellow?' asked the reporter, loosening his hold slightly, but making sure that Cunningham couldn't surprise him and make a dash to escape.

'The man I was following,' answered Cunningham, sitting up and rubbing his arm, for Anthony's grip had numbed it. 'You surely don't suppose that *I'm* the Black Hunchback, do you?'

Vyne looked at him searchingly. The sincerity in the young man's eyes was obviously not assumed, and after a few seconds' scrutiny, Anthony was convinced that whatever the explanation was Cunningham was acting straightforwardly.

'What's the idea of masquerading in this disguise?' he enquired, nodding at the black costume that Cunningham was wearing.

'If you'll let me get up, I'll tell you,' said Frank with a rueful smile. He struggled to his feet, followed by the reporter.

'Phew!' he exclaimed, stretching his strained muscles; 'that was a good grip you got on me! Have you got a cigarette? Mine are in my other clothes.'

Anthony handed him his case, and after Cunningham had lighted up, lit one himself.

'Now,' he said, puffing out a cloud of smoke, 'let's hear all about it.'

'Well,' began Cunningham, as they walked across the meadow side by side, 'after what Darrell told me about the attack on Pauline last night I made up my mind that tonight I'd do a bit of amateur detective work on my own. I thought there would be more chance of catching this fellow outside the house, than you would have from the inside. At first I thought of telling you my idea, but I was afraid that you might stop me if I did.'

'I certainly should have done,' interposed Vyne. 'You ran a very good risk of being shot!'

'Well, anyway,' continued Cunningham, 'I decided I wouldn't tell you. Then it struck me if I was seen by the police, or anyone lurking about round the Towers, I should have some difficulty in explaining my presence, so I hit upon what I thought was a really brilliant idea. I thought that if I made myself up to represent the Black Hunchback, even if I were seen by anyone, they wouldn't enquire into my identity too closely. I had this costume by me — a relic of some amateur theatricals I took part in last Christmas in the village. I slipped out by the back door, and made my way towards the Towers through Colethorpe Woods. I kept a sharp look-out, hoping to catch some glimpse of the real Black Hunchback, and, by Jove, I saw him!'

Anthony paused in his walk, a gleam in his eyes.

'You saw him!' he repeated quickly.

'Yes, but he wasn't disguised.'

'Would you recognise him again?' said the reporter, a trace of excitement in his voice.

Cunningham shook his head.

'No,' he replied disappointedly, 'I couldn't get near enough to see his face. I heard the sound of a shot while I was on my way to the Towers, and I was hurrying to find out what had happened when I suddenly spotted our friend hurrying away from the Home Covert. It was the furtiveness in his actions that first convinced me that he was the man I was seeking, so I decided to follow him and find out where he went to. And I believe I've discovered his hiding place — ' He broke off with a little gasp of pain.

'What's the matter?' asked Vyne quickly.

'I believe I've ricked my ankle,' answered the young man, 'when I fell in that hole in the meadow. It didn't hurt me just now, but it's beginning to ache like the deuce. Do you mind if we rest here for a moment, Mr. Vyne?'

They had arrived by the side of a broken wooden fence that divided the meadow from an adjoining ploughed field. Anthony agreed and they stopped. Frank hoisted himself on to the upper bar of the fence, while the reporter leaned against a post. In his black tights and leather jerkin, Cunningham presented a curious sight as he perched unsteadily on the narrow rail, like some strange and monstrous bird.

'You were saying,' prompted Anthony, 'that you had discovered the hiding place of our unknown assassin.'

'Yes,' answered the young man. 'I followed for some distance, and presently found that we were close to part of the Chiltern Hills. I don't know whether you know the country round about here well, but a few hundred yards beyond Colethorpe Woods, there is a disused gravel pit, and the man I was trailing was going directly for it.

'When he got to the edge of the pit,' continued Cunningham, 'which slopes slowly down to the bottom, although the other side rises sheer almost to the top of the hill, from the side of which it was originally excavated, he stopped and looked about him evidently to make sure that he was unobserved. After a few seconds he went on across the bottom of the pit towards the sheer side. The place had been in disuse for many years, and both the bottom and the sides have become thickly overgrown with bushes and shrubs. I saw him climbing among the bushes at the base of the opposite side, and then I lost sight of him altogether.' He paused.

'You didn't see where he went to?' asked Vyne, his brain working rapidly.

'No,' replied Frank, throwing away the stump of his cigarette. 'It seemed to me that he vanished behind a large clump of bushes about half way up the face of the hill.'

'Humph!' muttered Anthony, 'It looks as if there must be the entrance to a fissure or cave behind that screen of bushes. There's no reason for a man to climb half way up a sheer wall to hide himself behind a lot of bushes.'

'That's what I thought,' agreed Cunningham. 'In a minute or two he reappeared again, and proceeded to retrace his steps towards the Towers. I followed, but somewhere near the Home Covert I lost him. He completely disappeared. I hung about, hoping to find some trace of the man for some time, but without result, and I was going home when I caught sight of you. I immediately thought that it was my friend from the gravel pit, and when you started chasing me I don't mind confessing that I got scared and bolted.' He laughed as he concluded.

'So that's what happened,' said Anthony, smiling. 'I hope I didn't hurt you, but I had no idea it was you. I must congratulate you on a most important discovery. I shall take the first opportunity of investigating that gravel pit myself. In fact, as there's no time like the present I think I shall have a look round tonight.'

'For Heaven's sake, be careful,' urged

Cunningham. 'The man's a desperate and dangerous character.'

'I'm getting used to those sort of people,' said Anthony, with a grim little smile.

'I think I'd better come with you,' said the young man, as he slipped off the fence. As his injured foot touched the ground, however, he gave a gasp of pain, and would have fallen had not Vyne supported him.

'The best thing you can do, my friend, is to go straight home and go to bed, with a cold compress on that ankle of yours,' advised the reporter, 'and give up all idea of accompanying me. It's absolutely impossible, with your foot like that.'

And in spite of the young man's protestations, Anthony had his way. Leaning heavily on his arm, Cunningham allowed himself to be led towards his home. When they arrived at the gate Anthony persuaded the young man to direct him to the gravel pit.

After a great deal of argument, Frank gave way, and gave him the necessary instructions.

Vyne left him shortly after to hobble up

the short path to the front door, whilst the reporter himself bent his steps towards the gravel pit just under the shadow of the Chiltern Hills.

It was some distance from Cunningham's house, and Anthony found time to think over the events of the evening, and re-arrange his thoughts accordingly.

At any rate, one mystery had been cleared up — the identity of the mysterious tramp, whose presence had worried him for the reason that in no way would it fit into the theory which he had formed regarding the rest of the strange business. There still remained, however, the motive for his murder, and the reason for his presence in the rose garden. Was it possible that he had discovered the real identity of the Black Hunchback, and had been shot to ensure his silence?

That theory would account for the strange fact of his having followed his murderer into the rose garden, which Anthony had proved by the over-lapping footprints. If such were the case, it helped considerably the solution of the problem.

There remained the killing of Travis,

the disappearance of Sir Owen, and the attempted abduction of Pauline Langley, and Vyne flattered himself that he had discovered the solution to this part of the puzzle. He was confident that he knew the identity of the man masquerading as the Black Hunchback.

The photograph on the mantelpiece in the drawing room had given him his first clue, and the enquiries he had made in London had helped to strengthen his vague theory, even if they hadn't supplied any really definite proof.

As he strode along through the cool night air, Anthony felt that curious sense of elation which was always his when he saw the end of a particularly intricate piece of work in sight. It was not that he felt anything in the nature of personal triumph. Vyne viewed all his work from a perfectly impersonal point of view, and anything that approached conceit was abhorrent to his nature. Anyone who was not well acquainted with the man would have considered that his habit of keeping his theories and discoveries to himself was a form of conceit. But it was not so. It was the inherent trait of the artist which shrank from producing anything but the finished product. That was why Anthony tested all his theories and proved them up to the hilt before making them public property through the medium of his paper, and sometimes even Darrell remained in the dark as to the lines on which his friend was working, until Anthony had completed his case to his satisfaction.

But the stout man had got used to his friend's little ways, and unless Vyne was in the mood seldom questioned him. He knew that at the right time, and not a second before, the reporter would tell him everything.

After about twenty minutes' sharp walking, Anthony hove in sight of his destination. There was no mistaking the gravel pit. It lay carved out of the wooded hillside as if a lump had been taken out by a giant spoon. The bottom and sides were nearly covered by gorse and shrubs.

Anthony Vyne slowed up as he came near the lip of the sloping side that led to the bottom of the pit, and commenced to move down it slowly and cautiously, taking advantage of every vestige of cover that the place afforded.

He had no illusions concerning the type of man he was engaged in measuring swords with, and he was well aware that a life, more or less, meant nothing to the great unknown. He was already, to Anthony's knowledge, responsible for the killing of two men, and also an attempted murder — the shot at Vyne himself in the lane.

He reached the bottom of the pit, and paused to take stock of his surroundings. Ahead rose the sheer wall spoken of by Frank Cunningham, and half way up its surface Anthony saw the clump of bushes behind which Frank had said the man had disappeared. He saw something else now that he was nearer. At some time or other in the past a part of the hill top had fallen and formed a natural flight of rough steps leading almost up to the bushes.

Having ascertained this fact, Anthony started forward, again dodging from bush to bush until he reached the foot of the heap of rubble.

Here he listened intently. The night was intensely still, and not the faintest sound reached his straining ears. The whole world seemed at rest. The reporter started to climb the heap of fallen earth and stones. It was not so easy as it looked, and every now and then he had to take a stride that taxed even his long legs to reach the next foothold, but at last he arrived on a narrow ledge that ran behind the mass of bushes.

Again he stopped to listen. Not a sound disturbed the stillness. He crept along the ledge behind the bushes, and came upon a narrow opening in the face of the hillside. It was pitch black, and not more than about four feet wide. Anthony went cautiously inside, his arms extended so that he could touch the sides. He had gone about two yards when his groping fingers encountered only space. Evidently the passage widened into a larger opening inside. A faint sound caused him to swing round. At the same instant, something descended with crushing force on his head, and he fell like a log!

13

The Man Who Was Bound!

With a groan that got no further than his lips, but was choked back by the cruel gag that had been fastened in his mouth, Anthony Vyne came to his senses.

He was in pitch darkness, and his head ached and throbbed as though a thousand beaten anvils were in action inside his brain.

Presently, as his eyes became accustomed to the darkness, he saw that in front of him was a faint streak of cold grey light. He puzzled over this for a second or two before he realised that it was the first signs of dawn breaking outside the narrow entrance through which he had entered.

He tried turning his head, but the nauseating pain the movement caused, forced him to keep still. He closed his eyes again, and after a while began to feel better. His brain grew clearer, and he began to think. Someone had evidently been lying in wait for him in the darkness in the passage way. Either they had seen him as he crossed the gravel pit, or else followed him when he left Cunningham. Certainly, whoever it was, had been prepared for his coming. Anthony felt annoyed with himself for having walked so easily into the trap set for him.

As the pain in his head grew less, he commenced to take an interest in his surroundings, or as much of them as it was possible to see in the deep gloom which pervaded the whole place.

The light outside the opening was growing stronger, and part of it was beginning to filter through into the larger chamber in which the reporter lay. He tried to move his cramped limbs, and discovered that his arms and legs had been securely bound. Whoever had done the job had been an expert at the game, for Anthony found that, try as he would, he couldn't move an inch.

He lay still again, and let his eyes wander round him. They had grown used to the semi-darkness by now, and he was able to dimly make out some of the objects that surrounded him.

He was in a wide, low-roofed, cavern-like apartment, apparently hewn out of the solid hillside. How far back it extended, he was unable to determine, for that part was still shrouded in darkness.

Opposite to where Anthony lay, was a rough bed of clean straw, and one or two blankets folded beside it. Further on stood an old rotting box on which were several ends of candle, and scattered round this a collection of empty food tins. There was little doubt that this was the temporary abode of the unknown assassin.

Anthony wondered where he had gone to at the present time, and how long he was likely to be before he returned.

Just at that moment, the stillness was broken by the sound of a faint groan! It seemed to come from close behind him! Anthony tried to twist his head round, and after several futile efforts discovered that it was impossible. Again came the faint moaning sound.

Determined to catch a glimpse somehow

of the source from which the sound proceeded, the reporter started to roll his body round. It was a difficult task, bound as he was, but after some time he succeeded in moving in an arc for about four feet. It was now possible for Anthony to make out the other wall of the cave that had previously been behind him.

Lying close up against this was the figure of a man wrapped in some mauve coloured garment, and similarly bound and gagged. The reporter started, as the colour of the garment worn by the other supplied him with the clue to his identity. It was the missing Sir Owen!

Anthony's vague theory was receiving startling confirmation.

About two yards separated the reporter from Sir Owen Langley, and Anthony began to make every effort to decrease the distance. He suffered considerable discomfort and pain in his attempt, for the cords which bound him cut deeply into his flesh at every movement, but at last he attained his object and rolled his body along beside the other. Sir Owen was awake and conscious, for his eyes were wide open, and held an expression of astonishment in their depths as they focused themselves on the reporter.

Around the baronet's head was tied a blood-stained bandage. Anthony began to seek some means of communication. He tried to work the gag loose by moving his jaw, but it had been too securely tied.

At any moment the unknown masquerader might return, and then all chance of learning anything from Sir Owen would be gone.

He essayed a further attempt to loosen his bonds. He strained and tugged at the cords until his wrists were raw, and every muscle in his body ached, but without result. Then suddenly an idea struck him. Sir Owen's hands had been bound to his sides, and although the wrists were tightly secured the fingers were free. If he could so manoeuvre himself that the back of his head rested beside one of the baronet's hands — would it be possible for Sir Owen to undo the knot securing the gag?

The reporter decided to try, and again commenced his wriggling motion. Having got his head in the right position, the difficulty now was to make Sir Owen understand what was required of him. He raised his head, and tapped gently with the knot on the baronet's fingers. Sir Owen grasped the idea at once, for the reporter felt him begin to fumble at the knot. It was slow work, however, and Anthony's head began to ache again with the strain of keeping it in that unnatural position. He gave a sigh of relief as presently he felt the gag begin to loosen.

In a few minutes the knot was untied, and Anthony spat the gag from his mouth. His mouth was sore and his tongue swollen, so that it was several seconds before he could speak.

'Sir Owen,' he managed to croak at length, 'It's — I — Vyne.'

The baronet showed his recognition in the expression of his eyes.

'I'll try and see if I can untie your gag with my teeth,' he continued. 'Can you manage to turn over on your side away from me?'

Sir Owen nodded his head with difficulty and by a supreme effort succeeded in rolling over.

Anthony edged his way up until he was in the required position, and set to work on the knot with his strong white teeth.

He made short work with it, and in less than two minutes Sir Owen was free of the gag.

'Good heavens, Vyne,' he gasped huskily, when he found his voice, 'how the deuce did you get here?'

Anthony gave him a short account of his connection with the case.

'The infernal scoundrel,' interjected the baronet, as the reporter related the attempted abduction of Pauline. He didn't interrupt again until Anthony had finished his narrative.

'I'm afraid I'm responsible for the death of poor Travis, Vyne,' said Sir Owen, 'although I can assure you it was quite an accident.'

'He was in the shrubbery following the Black Hunchback when you fired. Your bullet missed the mark it was intended for, and struck Travis killing him instantly,' said Anthony promptly.

Sir Owen looked at him in astonishment.

'How did you know that?' he asked.

'It was just elementary deduction,' answered the reporter. 'The shot that killed the gamekeeper had certainly been fired from your automatic, which I found in the shrubbery. As soon as I knew that Travis had not been killed in the Home Covert but had been for some reason, conveyed thence after his death, and also knew that Miss Langley heard two shots on the night you disappeared, it was a simple matter to guess what had happened.

'Sir Owen, who is the man who has been masquerading as the Black Hunchback, and keeping you a prisoner here?'

The baronet was silent.

'I think I could make a fairly correct guess at his identity,' continued Anthony. 'And I assure you that the relationship between you should not be allowed to stand in the way of your doing all in your power to bring your brother-in-law to justice. Don't forget he is guilty of the worst crime of all — murder!'

'So you know?' groaned Sir Owen. 'Yes, you're quite right. It is my first wife's brother who is responsible for all this, and, as you say, I should not hesitate to aid in bringing him to the gallows. He richly deserves the extreme penalty of the law, for in addition to his other crimes, he nearly broke his sister's heart, and was partly to blame for her early death.'

Sir Owen paused and cleared his throat.

'I married my first wife, Mercia Fearon, when I was quite a young man,' he continued. 'I met her in the Argentine during the time I was attached to the Embassy out there, and a sweeter girl never lived. Even at that time her brother, Geoffrey, was giving her a lot of trouble on account of the wild life he was leading.

'We came to England shortly after our marriage, and I managed to get Geoffrey a fairly good job in a broker's office, and we hoped that he would steady down. But he quickly became mixed up with a lot of undesirable friends, and eight months later he was arrested for forgery. The shock coming at a time when my wife was in particularly delicate health, proved too great for her system and she died.'

There was a slight husky note in his

voice as he went on.

'As it was his first offence, Geoffrey Fearon got off with a light sentence. But he had not been out of prison long before he was again arrested, this time on a more serious charge — the robbery of the Western and Union Bank, and the attempted murder of the night watchman.'

'I remember the case,' interposed Anthony.

'Well, Fearon got a heavy sentence,' said Sir Owen. 'I must say that I was relieved, for while he was at large I felt a certain amount of responsibility.

'I married again shortly after, and settled down permanently at Langley Towers. I was always very interested in the legend of the treasure, and a few years ago I set to work to try and solve the meaning of the verse left behind by my ancestor, Sir Hugo, as a clue to its hiding place. Then suddenly, about a fortnight ago, I received a letter from Geoffrey Fearon, stating that he had been discharged from prison, and asking for a large sum of money.

'The address was somewhere in Bloomsbury, but I can't quite remember the street.'

A sudden quick gleam of interest lit up the grey depths of Anthony's eyes.

'Have you still got that letter?' he asked quickly.

'Yes,' answered the baronet. 'It's in the safe in my library, I sent him a small sum, but nothing like the amount he demanded, and suggested that the best thing he could do would be to leave the country. I got no reply. Three days ago, I suddenly stumbled on the solution of the treasure clue.

'It was quite late when I made my discovery, and I decided to put off the actual testing of my theory until the following day. When I got to bed, however, I found that I was too excited to sleep. For some time I lay tossing about, and at last decided to get up. I rose, and as I looked out of the window I saw someone moving about the shrubbery on the lawn. I thought that it might be a burglar, and seizing my pistol I rushed downstairs and out into the grounds. I ran to the shrubbery and saw a figure dressed in black, crouching among the rhododendrons.

'As I approached, it raised its arm, and I saw the moonlight gleam on a pistol barrel. I fired, and at the same moment there was a sharp cry, and a flash of flame from the other's weapon.

'Everything went black, and I remembered no more until I found myself in this place bound hand and foot, and Geoffrey Fearon bending over me!'

Sir Owen moistened his dry lips with his tongue before proceeding.

'The bullet that struck me had only grazed the side of my head. I asked Fearon what he was doing lurking about the Towers, and he told me that he had been in the vicinity for several days. And it appeared that for some reason or other he was in hiding. He demanded a large sum of money, and when I refused, told me that he intended to keep me a prisoner until I changed my mind. He knew all about my having been working on the clue of the treasure.'

'I wonder how he discovered that?' said Vyne.

'He said,' answered Sir Owen, 'that he overheard the chauffeur telling my butler that I had solved the meaning of the verse. As a matter of fact, I did say something of the sort to Merling the other day. It was no secret, everyone knew that I was hoping to find the bullion. Fearon said I'd better be sensible and tell him where the treasure was to be found, for no one would dream of looking for me here. He told me he had accounted for my disappearance by making it look as though I had murdered the gamekeeper. Fearon had found a little gold masonic charm in the pocket of my dressing gown, where I had thrust it one day after showing it to young Cunningham, and this he had put in the dead man's hand.'

'I knew it had been placed there after his death,' remarked Anthony, 'because the fingers were clasped round it quite limply and not tightly, as would have been the case if it had been snatched before death.'

'Ever since I've been here, Fearon has continually badgered me to tell him where the treasure is,' said Sir Owen. 'I had to tell him in the end.'

'What!' cried Anthony, 'you don't mean

to say he knows?'

'He threatened me with the alternative of either telling him, or seeing my daughter tortured before my eyes, and gave me twenty-four hours to think it over. The time expired about three hours ago. And I told him all I knew to save Pauline.'

'Why, even now he may be securing the bullion and making his getaway,' muttered Vyne, in a voice full of chagrin.

'No,' said the baronet, 'I could only tell him the clue to the hiding place of the treasure. I don't know myself where it is actually hidden. I never tested my theory.'

'What do you mean?' asked the reporter.

'Well,' the baronet replied, 'the verse runs:

' 'The arrow from the bow released
In one direction, only goes
Be it North, South, West or-East,
But not from where the wind blows,
Where at length it comes to rest,
Seek there, and ye shall find in chest.'

'After I had tried every conceivable means of finding hidden words, acrostics or cryptograms, it suddenly occurred to me to take the literal meaning of the words. On looking at it from this point of view, I came to the conclusion that the meaning was fairly simple. It merely meant the discharge of an arrow from a bow from such a position that it could only travel in one direction. Now the line: 'But not from where the wind blows' — can only mean from somewhere in a sheltered position, the most probable place being from somewhere inside Langley Towers.'

Anthony murmured an agreement. Sir Owen's reasoning was perfectly clear and concise.

'It puzzled me for a long time,' the baronet went on, 'as to where this could possibly be, for obviously the arrow must travel in a dead straight line for it to be possible to indicate the exact point where the treasure lay hidden. If it even deviated a few inches at its starting point, it could land at the end of its flight anywhere within a radius of several hundred yards, which would be altogether too vague. The only way I could think of was that it was fired through some kind of narrow aperture in which it just fitted, similar to a bullet in a gun barrel. Then if this aperture had a fixed locality, every arrow that was fired through it would, of necessity, travel and strike every time in the exact same spot. Do you follow me?'

'Perfectly,' replied Vyne. 'I think you have worked it out most ingeniously, and I feel sure that it is the correct solution.'

'I next set about discovering anything in the house that at all fitted in with this idea, and after a long search, I found in the wall of the room at the top of the North Tower a long tube-like hole about two inches in circumference. It penetrated the entire thickness of the wall, which is about eighteen inches, and slanted downwards. It had been plugged with a wooden plug the same colour as the interior of the room and was practically invisible. I'm convinced, Anthony, that an arrow shot through this aperture will land at the spot where the treasure is hidden.'

'And Fearon possesses this information?' said Vyne, and it was more of a statement than a question.

'He can't use his knowledge until after dark tonight,' replied the baronet. 'It would be too risky. He has got to break into the house to get to the room in the Tower.'

'In the meantime, we are in a particularly nasty position,' said Anthony. 'You can't loosen those cords, I suppose?'

'I've tried again, and again,' answered Sir Owen. 'They are much too securely tied.'

'Humph!' muttered the reporter. 'I wonder if I could work the knots loose with my teeth? I believe I could, and so long as Fearon keeps away until we are free, we stand a chance of putting a spoke in his wheel yet.'

Without any loss of time he started to put his scheme into practice, and commenced work on the ropes that bound the baronet's hands. For five minutes he worked, but without shifting the tight knot one iota.

The cord used was thin but as tough as steel, and the knot might have been welded together for all the impression Anthony made on it. He tried at length to bite through the strands, and this proved a little more successful, and he had partially succeeded in gnawing through one strand, when there came a sharp exclamation from the narrow entrance to the cave, and the next instant Geoffrey Fearon stood before them!

He was a man of medium height, broad-shouldered, and might have been described as good-looking, but for the fact that his eyes were small and set too close to the thin nose.

He was carrying a parcel, but as he saw what was happening he dropped it with a muttered oath, and pulled Anthony Vyne roughly away from Sir Owen.

'I appear to have arrived just in time,' he remarked, with a grim smile. 'Half-an-hour later, and I should have found that the birds had flown from the nest.'

He stooped and examined the ropes that bound Sir Owen with a critical eye, to see the extent of the damage Vyne had done.

'I'm afraid that I shall have to take steps to clip your wings once and for all,' he continued, straightening up. 'If it hadn't been for this infernal meddler' — he shot a malevolent glance at Anthony — 'I might have been disposed to let you free — after I had secured the treasure, of course. But he knows too much, and now it would be confoundedly risky.'

'What do you intend to do with us?' asked Anthony quietly.

Fearon chuckled.

'Dead men tell no tales,' he quoted pleasantly. 'Have patience, and you'll see. I don't think I'll trouble to gag you again. You could shout your head off here, and no one could hear you. That's one of the pleasant little properties of this place, which makes it such an admirable summer residence.'

He spoke in a quiet conversational tone of voice, and might quite easily have been discussing the weather or the latest news in the papers, but for the expression of his eyes. They were hard and cold and merciless, and there lurked in their pale blue depths a look of such inhuman cruelty, that in spite of himself Anthony Vyne felt a little shiver chase down his spine.

'I tried to get you once, Vyne,' the man continued, as he proceeded to unpack the parcel he had brought in with him. 'I missed you that time. You can bet your sweet life that I shan't make a second blunder.'

The contents of the parcel he laid out upon the top of the wooden box. They consisted of what looked like a large cigar, and a coil of thin, white blind cord

'This pleasantly situated residence, with every modern convenience,' continued Fearon lightly, 'will shortly be for sale, including fixtures — isn't that how the agents put it? You two constitute the fixtures.'

He lighted a cigarette, and smoked for a time in silence.

Anthony had recognised the objects on the box, and his skin went cold and clammy as he realised the diabolical intention of the man. Outwardly, however, he remained calm and unmoved

Presently Fearon finished his cigarette, and produced a small brown leather bag from a corner. Opening it he quickly ran through the contents as if to satisfy himself that he had forgotten nothing. Then he closed it with a snap, and came over to where Anthony and Sir Owen lay.

'I shall be leaving here shortly,' he announced, 'for good, and I shan't be sorry. So if either of you have got anything to say, you'd better say it — quickly.'

'Fearon,' said Anthony steadily 'Why did you shoot the tramp?'

'Do you mean 'Soapy' Davis?' asked Geoffrey Fearon.

'So you knew him, did you?' said Vyne.

'Yes, I knew him,' replied Fearon, 'and if he hadn't known me he might have been alive now. He was in the next cell to mine on the 'Moor,' the blackmailing little tyke.'

'Oh, that was it, was it?' said Anthony softly, 'he tried to blackmail you?'

'That was it, agreed the man. 'You can't say that I'm not doing all I can to help you. Davis recognised me on one of my nocturnal excursions when I was not dressed as the Black Hunchback, and threatened to give me away. So he died among the roses,' he added flippantly. 'Is there anything else you would like to know?'

'Quite a lot,' answered Anthony. 'But I'll reserve that until I meet you again — at the Old Bailey!'

'There's going to be no Old Bailey for me,' said Fearon, 'or for you, for that matter. When you leave here, which will be very soon, you'll leave for good — via the roof!' He chuckled softly. 'Well, I'm wasting time with all this gossip,' he went on, 'and I've got quite a lot to do.'

He crossed to the broken box, and picked up the cigar-shaped object and the coil of white stuff.

Coolly and without haste, he proceeded to measure off a length of the string-like substance, and taking a penknife from his pocket, cut it at the place he had marked.

Anthony watched him with an indescribable feeling in his heart. He knew, only too well, what these preparations portended, and unless both he and Sir Owen could manage to get free of the bonds that bound them, they would in a short while be face to face with a terrible death!

'I've always thought that blasting was an interesting subject,' remarked Fearon at length, as he proceeded to fix the white cord to the cylinder. 'Of course, we did a lot of it in the stone quarries at Princetown, and it always fascinated me. But I never got a chance of studying the operation at close quarters. That is a pleasure which will shortly be yours, and I think you ought to thank me for giving you the opportunity of witnessing such an interesting experiment.

Vyne remained silent. It was useless talking to this cold-blooded scoundrel, who could joke in the act of preparing for the perpetration of a fiendish murder. For murder it was.

Geoffrey Fearon disappeared into a dark corner of the cave, carrying the instrument of death and destruction with him, and they could hear the sound of scraping and the rattling tinkle of falling stones. In a little while, the man re-appeared, trailing the string-like material behind him. It reached to the centre of the cave, and he dropped the end almost opposite the reporter and Sir Owen.

'And that's that!' he said, in his pleasant conversational voice; 'I have only now to light the fuse, and in about three-quarters of an hour 'Hey Presto!' — you will both have vanished, and become particles of dust floating in the air!'

You damned swine!' burst out the baronet, as he realised for the first time the diabolical intention of the man. 'You intend to blow us to pieces!'

Fearon looked down at him, smiling.

'You've guessed right first time; really, your intelligence is quite brilliant,' he answered. 'I feel sure that Vyne knew all about it directly I unpacked the things from my parcel. Didn't you?'

He evidently expected no reply, for he hurried away, at once, and commenced to examine the mechanism of an automatic pistol which he took from his pocket. Apparently satisfied, he slipped up the safety catch and put it back again. Then he looked at his watch.

'Seven o'clock,' he remarked. 'I must be off. I think if you don't mind, I'll just slip those gags on again. Unless anyone came within two yards of the opening to this sumptuous abode they wouldn't hear you if you shouted your heads off, but I can't afford to take any risks.'

He bent over the reporter, and with deft fingers reaffixed the gag which he took from the floor by his side.

Anthony's fingers itched to get at the man, but he was helpless. Something of his thoughts must have communicated themselves to Fearon, for he smiled sardonically into Vyne's upturned face.

'You'd give anything to have your hands free, wouldn't you?' he asked with a chuckle. 'I am really sorry I can't oblige you.'

He turned from Anthony and repeated the operation with Sir Owen.

'There!' he said, as he straightened up, 'I think everything's in order now.'

He picked up the brown leather bag, and took a last look round the cave. Then he put the bag down again. 'I was almost forgetting the most important part of the programme,' he said with a chuckle

He took a box of matches from his pocket, struck one, and applied the flame to the end of the fuse. It spluttered furiously and the acrid smell of burning powder came to Anthony's nostrils.

Fearon replaced the matches, picked up the bag again, and walked over towards the narrow opening, but on the threshold he paused.

'Goodbye, gentlemen,' he cried, waving his hand. 'I wish you both a pleasant journey!'

14

Darrell Gets Anxious

After Anthony had left him on the lawn, Darrell returned to the house with Hume. The old man looked white and ill, and was evidently suffering acutely from the tragic discovery of his son's dreadful death.

They entered the house by the back door, and the butler, with a word of apology to the stout man, proceeded at once to his own room.

Jack understood and could sympathise with the old man's feelings. After all, whatever Soapy Davis may have been, and apparently it was obvious he had been a thorough bad lot, Hume still looked upon him as the little chap he had often nursed upon his knee.

Darrell's heart was full of sympathy for the butler, as he made his way back to the drawing room in search of Pauline Langley.

The girl was waiting anxiously for news.

She had obeyed Anthony Vyne's instructions and remained in the room, although greatly against her inclination, for she was consumed with curiosity to know the meaning of the shot.

At Jack's entrance, she poured forth a flood of questions, and Darrell gave her a brief account of what had happened, omitting, however, to mention that the tramp had been identified or that he was any relation of the old butler.

'It seems as if some dreadful curse had been put upon the place,' said Pauline, when he had finished. 'First, poor daddy's disappearance, then the death of Travis, and now this last tragedy. What can be the meaning of it all?'

To be perfectly truthful, Darrell was as much puzzled as she was, but he didn't say so.

'I expect the solution will prove to be quite simple when we know it,' he replied.

'Where's Mr. Vyne?' she asked.

'He's making some further investigations in the rose garden,' answered Jack;

'He'll be back soon now, I expect.'

But he little guessed at the time how many hours were to pass before he saw his friend again!

For some time they sat and talked over the events of the last two or three days, and the soft-toned clock on the mantel-piece chimed eleven before they became aware of the lateness of the hour.

The girl looked up as the sound reached her ears.

'Good gracious! I'd no idea it was as late as that,' she cried. 'What can have happened to Mr. Vyne?'

Darrell felt a faint twinge of uneasiness creep over him, but tried not to let it become visible to the girl.

'Oh, I expect he's all right,' he replied, reassuringly. 'He has a habit of disappearing for hours when he's puzzling things out. I'll stroll down to the rose garden, and see if I can see any sign of him.'

He rose to his feet.

'I think I shall go to bed,' said Pauline. 'Frank said he would come over this evening, but he hasn't turned up. I telephoned a little while ago, but they said he was out. I wonder where he can be?'

'Perhaps he had gone down to the village for something or other, and got detained until it was too late to call,' suggested Jack.

'Well, he might have 'phoned, anyhow,' said the girl, and the stout man conceded a smile at the tone of her voice. It was obvious that she was considerably piqued at the young man's neglect.

Darrell said good night to Pauline, and started to make his way to the rose garden.

But there was no sign of Anthony.

'Where can he have got to?' thought Darrell. Had he suddenly discovered some clue, and was he following it up while it was still fresh? The stout man felt slightly aggrieved. He hated to be left out of his friend's investigations, and the prospect of aimlessly wandering around and cooling his heels with nothing more exciting in view than bed to follow, did not appeal to his adventurous nature in the slightest. It was too bad of Anthony to go off like this and leave him behind.

At any rate, he determined on one

thing — he wouldn't go to bed until Vyne had come in, and he had learned if possible where he had been. Darrell mentally made the proviso 'if possible,' because Anthony had a disconcerting habit of being as dumb as an oyster with regard to his movements on these occasions.

The night was very still and quiet, and the moonlight touched the scene like a magic brush held in the hand of a giant artist, tracing the landscape in burnished silver against the deep fathomless blue of the sky. But Darrell was not in the mood for quiet. He wanted excitement, and the stillness of the night only annoyed him. He felt too restless to go in yet, and continued his stroll round the grounds, half hoping that he might come across the lurking figure of the Black Hunchback to enliven up the proceedings — but he saw nobody.

There was a light in Pauline's bedroom, but shortly this went out, leaving the house a mass of complete darkness.

Jack Darrell tried to concentrate his mind on the case, and would weave some theory that would account for all the facts in his possession, but after turning and twisting it over and over again until his brain felt weary, he failed to arrive at any satisfactory conclusion.

A clock in the village struck twelve as he found himself back at the side door of the house. He felt a return of that slight uneasiness that he had experienced before. Had something happened to Anthony? It seemed unlikely that he was still searching for clues at this hour. It was over three hours ago since he had left Darrell on the lawn to return to the rose garden, and he had said that he wouldn't be long.

Darrell pushed gently on the door expecting it to open to his touch, but it didn't — it was locked!

He guessed at once what had happened. The household had concluded that he had gone to bed and locked up. He remembered the French windows leading from the drawing room to the terrace, and made his way round to the steps. He found the window had been fastened when he got there, but he soon slipped back the catch with the long blade of his penknife. He entered the room, closed the windows, and crossing to the door switched on the electric light. He was beginning to get seriously worried now over the continued absence of Anthony, and as his uneasiness increased his irritability decreased in proportion.

All sorts of visions crowded into his chaotic mind. He pictured his friend in every kind of perilous situation, but, curiously enough, he never came within miles of imagining the true one.

Hour after hour. Dawn began to show faintly in the eastern sky, and the cold light filtering through the windows showed his face drawn and haggard, and his eyes heavy with want of sleep.

The clock on the mantelpiece chimed six, and as the last faint sound throbbed to silence, Darrell made up his mind to have another look round outside, and see if — now that it was light — he could pick up any trace of Anthony. Anything was better than this nerve-destroying inaction, this futile helpless waiting.

He had just crossed to the French windows, when suddenly on the silence of the still sleeping house, came the sharp shrill summons of the telephone bell in the hall. Jack was across the room in almost two strides, and had jerked the door open; in another two strides he had reached the instrument.

Of course, it was Anthony ringing up. It couldn't be anyone else at this hour. All his fears had been groundless, after all. With a light heart, he lifted the receiver off its hook, expecting to hear the well-known tones of his friend's voice speaking.

But he was doomed to disappointment. The voice over the wire was Frank Cunningham's!

'Hello!' said the young man: 'Who is that?' 'It's Darrell,' answered the stout man; 'what is it?'

'Oh, is that you, Mr. Darrell?' cried Cunningham. 'You're up early, aren't you? Is Mr. Vyne about yet?'

'He hasn't been back all night,' said Jack. 'I'm getting anxious about him. I haven't been to bed yet.'

'I'm anxious about him, too,' said Cunningham. 'That's why I risked waking the house by ringing up so early. I haven't slept very well, and I've been worrying all night about Mr. Vyne.'

'Why?' asked Darrell. 'Do you know where he went to?'

'Yes,' replied Cunningham; 'at least, I know where he was going when he left me.'

He related to Jack what had happened on the previous evening, when Anthony had chased him through the wood.

'He insisted upon my going to bed,' concluded the young man, 'although I tried to persuade him to let me go with him. But he wouldn't hear of it. I do hope nothing has happened.'

'I'm afraid it has,' said Darrell gravely. 'Where is this gravel pit?'

'If you're thinking of going there, let me come with you,' said Cunningham, 'my ankle's much better now.'

'All right,' replied Jack, 'where shall I pick you up?'

'You've got to pass my place to get there, unless you take a short cut through the woods, and if you don't know the way you'll probably lose yourself.'

He told the fat man quickly how to get to his house.

'I'm coming along now,' said Darrell.

'I'll be ready,' replied Cunningham, 'and wait for you at the gate.'

'Have you got a gun?' asked Jack.

Cunningham replied in the negative.

'All right,' continued Darrell, 'I'll bring one for you along with me.'

He banged the receiver back on the rest, and raced up the stairs to his room. Flinging back the lid of his suitcase, he snatched out a brace of automatics, pausing only long enough to satisfy himself that the mechanism was in working order.

Dashing down the stairs again, he tore out of the house via the drawing room windows. He was certain now that Anthony had fallen into a trap, and his great anxiety was whether he would be in time to save him.

In spite of the handicap of his size and weight, Darrell covered the two miles that separated Langley Towers from Cunningham's residence as if he were competing for a cross country race.

Frank Cunningham was as good as his

word, and was waiting at the gate when Darrell arrived panting and perspiring. The stout man scarcely stopped as Cunningham joined him, but hurriedly passed him one of the automatics, and together they hurried on towards the disused gravel pit.

Cunningham's handsome face wore a look of anxiety as he limped along beside Jack. His ankle, although considerably better, still pained him, but he set his teeth and kept up the hot pace set by his companion.

They wasted little breath in talking, for neither had much to say, their minds were too busily occupied in wondering what they should find at the end of their journey.

There was a sinking sick sensation in the region of Darrell's capacious stomach as he thought of all the hours that Anthony had been away. Anything might have happened during that time.

In a very short while, considering the distance, they came in sight of the gravel pit.

The sun was well up by now, and the

place lay silent and deserted beneath its rays.

Darrell slowed up.

'We've got to go carefully now,' he whispered hoarsely, 'or we may do more harm than good. Where did you say the bushes were behind which the man vanished?'

Cunningham pointed them out

Cautiously, followed by the young man, Jack made his way down into the pit, and to anyone watching, it would have seemed curious how closely he followed the movements of his friend on the preceding night.

Advancing warily and stopping every second to listen intently, they presently came to the bottom of the heap of fallen hillside that led up to the cave. Here Darrell stopped.

'I'm going up,' he whispered close to Cunningham's ear, 'you'd better stay here.'

Drawing his pistol from his pocket in readiness, he proceeded to climb slowly and laboriously up the mound. He found it more difficult than Anthony had done, for his stride was naturally much shorter. But he managed it without a sound, and found himself at length standing outside the narrow opening to the cave.

With a thumping heart he peered into the dark interior. A whiff of acrid smoke was wafted to his nose as he did so. He sniffed gently. It seemed as if a pistol had been fired recently, and a wave of sinking fear filled Darrell's whole being. What was he about to find in that dark and tomb-like opening?

He edged his way further in and listened. Not a sound! Coming in out of the sunlight, the darkness was intense, and at first he could see nothing. Then suddenly over in the blackness, he made out a winking spark of reddish fire. Still holding the automatic in his right hand, he felt in his pocket for his matches with his left. Putting the box in the palm of his right hand so that it didn't interfere with his pistol, the stout man extracted a match and lit it.

As the feeble yellow flame flared up, he took a hasty glance round, and almost at once espied the two bound and gagged figures lying side by side over against the opposite wall. Slipping the pistol into his pocket, he hurried over, and by the light of the half-burned match saw that the nearest one was Anthony Vyne.

Quickly Darrell whipped out his pocket knife and cut through the gag, tearing it from the reporter's mouth.

'Thank Heaven!' gasped Anthony fervently. 'Quick, old chap, cut through these cords and Sir Owen's. You haven't a moment to lose — the cartridge may explode at any moment!'

In a flash, Darrell's keen brain realised the meaning of the acrid smoke and the spark of red light, and working with feverish haste, his eyes now becoming accustomed to the gloom, he slashed through the bonds that bound Anthony and Sir Owen. They had to call to Cunningham to help to get the baronet out, for his limbs were helpless due to his long confinement in one position. While they were so engaged, Anthony went over to the spluttering fuse. Scarcely four inches remained!

'Hurry up, Darrell, old man!' he urged.

'If we are quick, we can get away. I am particularly anxious, for reasons which are obvious, for the explosion to take place as it was planned.'

They had some difficulty in getting the baronet down the rough way leading from the cave to the ground but, supported between Anthony and Frank they managed to accomplish it safely, and once on firm ground they hurried away as fast as they could from the scene of the horrible end that Fearon had planned for them both.

Scarcely had they all reached the further side of the gravel pit when there came a sudden dull boom!

The hillside shook and then slowly collapsed, until nothing remained but a heap of boulders and tumbled earth over which, like a pall, hung an immense cloud of white dust!

15

A Waiting Game

Feeling little the worse for his terrifying experience, Anthony was seated some two hours later in the Library at Langley Towers reading a long telegram that had been delivered that morning. It was from his agent in London, and was in answer to the wire that he had despatched earlier.

The reporter's face wore an expression of satisfaction as he perused the several sheets. He looked up as Darrell entered the room.

'Well, what's the next move?' asked his friend, rubbing his podgy hands.

'The next move,' answered Anthony, 'is for you to go down to the village, if you will, old chap, and send a wire to Hallam.'

He took a pencil from his pocket, and scribbled swiftly for a moment, then passed the paper over to his friend. Jack glanced at it. It was brief, but to the point.

* * *

'Come down at once Langley Towers. Leave train at preceding station and walk from there. Important discovery.

'VYNE.'

Darrell chuckled as he read it.

'I bet old Hallam will bless you by the time he's walked four miles along a hot and dusty road. It must be quite that from Little Camberley,' he said.

'A trifle more, I should say,' answered Anthony, with a twinkle in his eyes, 'but Hallam doesn't get much chance for exercise, and it will do him good.'

'I don't suppose he'll think so,' retorted Jack.

Anthony smiled.

'We none of us know what is good for us,' he remarked sententiously. 'Be careful you're not seen entering the post office when you take that by any strangers.'

Jack nodded. 'Trust me,' he replied, and waddled away.

For some time after he had gone away, Anthony Vyne sat motionless lost in thought. He was engaged in making his plans for the final scene of the problem, and in marshalling together all his facts. A faint smile curled the corners of his mouth, as he thought of the surprise he held up his sleeve for Hallam.

Fearon would, of course, as Anthony intended he should, imagine that both he and the baronet had perished in the explosion, and carry out his intention of collecting the treasure that night. And he would find Anthony ready to receive him.

Sir Owen had gone straight to his room and to bed on his return home. The strain of his long captivity and the lack of food, for Fearon had been sparing, and the baronet had only been given a small quantity of bread with a piece of tinned meat once each day, had left him very weak.

Pauline had been overjoyed at the return of her father, and the look she had given Anthony as she thanked him had set his pulses thrilling, and made him wish that no such person as Frank Cunningham existed. She was now sitting with her father, and the reporter was glad, for it would keep her out of the way during his preparations for the forthcoming night.

The entire staff had been ordered to remain indoors, for Anthony did not want to run the risk of losing his man, and a chance word dropped might easily reach the ears of Fearon, and once he knew that Anthony had escaped from the cave, he would be on his guard, and all hope of his coming to collect the treasure would be gone for ever.

With the end of the affair in sight, the reporter sat on thinking, comfortably ensconced in one of the deep library armchairs. It was going to be a big scoop for *The Messenger*. He could do little more now until the arrival of Hallam and nightfall. It would be well past midnight before Fearon would make an appearance — of that he was certain.

Cunningham had returned home after securing Anthony's promise to let him be in at the death, and was coming back to Langley Towers in time for dinner.

Feeling at peace with the world, Anthony searched in his pocket for a cigarette, and lighting it, puffed out a cloud of blue smoke with a sigh of contentment. And so the first part of the day passed peacefully enough.

Detective-Inspector Hallam arrived just before his time, hot and dusty, covered with perspiration, and blowing and grunting like a grampus.

'Enjoy your walk?' enquired Darrell, as he and Anthony met him in the hall.

'It's nearly killed me,' puffed the Inspector, as he scrubbed at his bristly hair with a large silk handkerchief. 'Now, what's it all about, Vyne? It'll have to be something damnably important to make up for that five-mile tramp.'

'It is,' said Anthony; 'I think you'll agree that it's very important when you know.'

They carried off the worthy Inspector for a wash, and presently returned to the Terrace, where tea was waiting. Hallam was introduced to Pauline, but the girl didn't remain long, excusing herself, and returning to her father's bedside.

When they were alone, Anthony told Hallam the story of the Black Hunchback. When Anthony came to the conclusion, Hallam looked at him enquiringly.

'It's an interesting business, Vyne,' he

said, 'but I'm hanged if I can see what you want me down for. Surely the local police could have helped you capture this man Fearon.'

'Certainly they could,' replied Anthony, with a smile. 'It's something entirely different that I want you for.'

'What?' demanded Hallam, sipping his third cup of tea.

'You'll see in good time,' answered the reporter.

'Humph!' grunted the Inspector, who had recovered somewhat, after his tea and wash, from the effects of the five-mile walk, and was in a good humour. 'I suppose that means that you're not going to tell me anything more? Well, I don't suppose you'd have brought me all the way down here for nothing, so I must wait and see.'

'You'll find it worth waiting for, Hallam, I assure you,' replied Anthony.

'I suppose you've dropped the Harper murder?' enquired the Inspector, later.

'I've made one or two enquiries,' said Anthony, shrugging his shoulders.

'He was a 'fence',' stated Hallam. 'We suspected it for years, although we hadn't got any definite proof. We found enough though when we went through his belongings. I shouldn't be surprised if North wasn't one of his clients.'

'By the way,' interrupted Anthony, 'how long was North staying at Harper's flat?'

'About three weeks,' answered Hallam.

'Where did he come from? Where was he living before?' asked the reporter

'Nobody knows,' said Hallam, with a grunt, running his fingers through his hair, a great habit of his. 'Good Heavens! We've made enough enquiries, but he just seems to have appeared from nowhere — out of thin air!'

Anthony became suddenly silent, gazing across the top of the pine trees that waved gently in the light breeze. Presently he roused himself, and suggested a game of billiards.

Hallam agreed, and they made their way to the billiard room, and spent the time till dinner was announced, knocking the balls about, while Darrell acted as marker.

Jack was intensely curious to learn the reason for Hallam's presence. Anthony had told him the story of Geoffrey Fearon, but try as he would the fat man could see no reason for bringing the worthy Inspector into it.

'I wonder what the devil Anthony's got up his sleeve,' he murmured to himself during the game. 'I've never known him do anything yet without a good reason, so I suppose there's something in it.'

Dinner was a silent meal. Pauline, at Sir Owen's request, had dined upstairs with her father. Frank Cunningham arrived just as they sat down, and he and Hallam made several ineffective attempts to start the ball of conversation rolling, but Anthony was in an abstracted mood, and seemed lost in a world of his own.

As darkness fell, Darrell began to feel a glow of excitement steal over him, and happening once to catch a glance of Cunningham, saw that he was in a similar condition.

The hours dragged slowly by on leaden feet. There was nothing to do, and everyone was too wrapped up in what was to come to be capable of thinking or taking any interest in side issues. At eleven o'clock

Anthony called them over to him.

'We shall take up our positions in the top room of the North Tower, the place from which the arrow has to be fired to point the spot where the treasure is hidden,' he said quietly.

'I wonder where the hiding place really is,' interjected Darrell

'I know, old chap,' answered Anthony surprisingly, 'I tested Sir Owen's theory this morning.'

'What!' cried Jack, disgustedly, 'and you never told me! You call yourself a friend! Where on earth did you get an arrow from?'

'I didn't use an arrow,' answered the reporter; 'I used a rifle, which I got from the gun room. Anything that fires in a straight line does equally as well as an arrow.'

'Where is the hiding place?' demanded Jack.

'You'll know presently,' replied Anthony.

Hallam grunted.

'Everything seems to be going to happen presently,' he remarked sarcastically.

'You're quite right, Hallam,' said

Anthony smiling blandly. 'It is! Come on,' he added, 'it's time we were taking up our positions. I have chosen the room in the Tower because our friend, Fearon is certain to make direct for that point. But what part of the house he will choose to break in, it's impossible to say. The room is being used as a lumber store, so there are plenty of places for concealment.'

He led the way towards the corridor while he was talking, which, running the entire length of the house, communicated between the two Towers, the hall merely forming a larger chamber in the centre. At the end of the corridor a flight of stone steps led upwards to the top of the Tower; at the side of these, on narrow landings, were four stout oak doors, one above the other. Anthony switched on an electric torch. The lower doors were locked and barred, but the topmost door stood ajar.

'There is no need for us to lock this door,' said Anthony, pausing outside it. 'The fact of its being open will not alarm Fearon. He will merely think that it had been left unlocked by Sir Owen the last time he was up here.'

They entered the large store room, which occupied the entire width of the Tower, except for the space taken up by the stairway.

It was dark and gloomy, for there was only a narrow slit in the thick outer wall that did duty for a window.

Anthony swept the light of his torch round, taking care to keep the rays from falling so that they could be seen from outside by anyone who might be watching. The place was half full of old packing cases and lumber of all description, and was thick with dust and cobwebs.

'I'm afraid we shall not be able to smoke,' said the reporter. 'The smell would put him on his guard.'

They selected positions as comfortable as possible behind the stacks of lumber, and Anthony switched off the torch. Through the partly opened door came the sound of the clock in the hall, faintly as though from a great distance, striking half-past eleven. And so in dead silence and pitch darkness they awaited the coming of the Black Hunchback!

16

In the North Tower

An hour passed slowly by. To Darrell, his nerves keyed to a tremendous pitch of excitement, it seemed the longest hour he had ever spent in his life. The deep, heavy breathing of Detective Inspector Hallam was the only sound that broke the intense silence. The darkness was like black velvet — impenetrable, save for a faint, almost invisible greyness which marked the slit-like window.

Presently a whispered question from Hallam reached Anthony's ears.

'How long do you imagine we shall have to wait here?' he rumbled, somewhere down in his boots.

'I've not the faintest idea,' answered the reporter, his voice scarcely audible.

'Because I'm getting cramp,' continued Hallam in a pained voice.

Darrell suppressed a chuckle quickly,

but not quickly enough, for it reached the ears of the Inspector, and he snorted wrathfully.

'It may seem funny to you,' he muttered, 'but you're younger than I am. It's a very trying position for a man of my age.

'Sh-s-sh!' warned Anthony; 'your whisper, I should think, could be heard several miles away, Hallam.'

Hallam grunted and relapsed into silence.

The wind had risen with the setting of the sun, and they could hear it sighing in the trees and round the corners of the house, whilst every now and again a cold breath entering through the narrow window, which was unglazed, played round the room and caused the watchers to shiver slightly.

The weather was changing, and there was the promise of rain in the air. The intense, almost tropical, heat of the past few days was evidently going to be succeeded by a spell of wet.

Another hour dragged by, and they heard one o'clock strike in a muffled tone from the hall clock, but still everything remained silent.

It was impossible to guess at what time Fearon would make his appearance, but Anthony had conjectured that it would be somewhere between twelve and two o'clock. It began to get light shortly after three, and it would be risky for the man to leave it too late. The slit-like window was becoming more visible now as the moon came round from the other side of the Tower, and showed up a pale streak in the otherwise intense darkness.

The half hour struck. Still nothing happened. Anthony possessed a tremendous amount of patience, but this game of waiting, with every sense strained to the uttermost, was sufficient to try the strongest nerves.

Again and again his imagination played tricks with him, and he found himself straining his ears to catch some faint sound, which afterwards he discovered was merely the rustling of the leaves outside, but that his overstraining ears had twisted into the semblance of a soft and stealthy footfall. Twice he had been caught by the sound of Hallam gently shifting his position as he tried to relieve his cramped limbs. Slowly, deadly slowly, the minutes dragged by. Anthony's eyes began to ache through staring fixedly into the darkness. The three-quarters struck.

Suddenly the reporter drew in his breath with a sharp hiss. From somewhere below in the silent house had come a faint sound! A slight clink of metal against metal!

Tensely Anthony waited, scarcely breathing, listening with straining ears for some further indication to tell him that the moment he had been waiting for, for so long, was near at hand.

But nothing further occurred. No other sound broke the silence. What seemed like an eternity passed without anything happening.

Anthony was beginning to think that his ears had again played him false when all at once there came the sound of a faint footfall!

It was the noise of someone moving slowly and stealthily up the stone stairway!

Geoffrey Fearon had arrived at last!

Anthony knew that the others had also heard it by the sudden cessation in the sound of their breathing.

The noise ceased. Fearon had stopped. A minute went by, and then the shuffling step became audible again, and this time continued until the intruder paused outside the partly open door!

There came the slight creak of a rusty hinge as the heavy door was swung further open, and the reporter sensed the presence of another person in the room!

A shaft of light sprang into being emanating from a torch held in the hand of the new arrival, and stabbed the darkness of the room. The light darted hither and thither, and its beams reflected from the light stone walls revealed a dim, black clad figure, its face concealed by a white silk handkerchief, half crouching as it moved. The figure of the Black Hunchback!

Fearon had donned his masquerade for this last adventure. The ray of light went probing about the room until it finally stopped and focused on a spot in the wall beside the narrow opening: a small, round hole in the stone, some two inches in circumference.

Fearon uttered a little murmur of satisfaction. He rested the torch upon the top of a packing case — the very case behind which Anthony crouched, and produced from somewhere beneath his strange black costume, a bow and arrow. And then Anthony acted!

With a shout to the others, he sprang in one flying leap over the packing case, and landed by the side of the startled figure in black. Fearon dropped the bow and arrow, and almost at the same instant that the reporter landed, snatched from one of his pockets an automatic pistol. There came a sharp crack and a spurt of orange flame, and a bullet whizzed past Anthony's ear, and hit the wall behind with a thud! Fearon had shot at close range!

It was a miracle that the shot missed, but it did, and before the other could fire again, Anthony had grappled with him, twisting the weapon from his hand, and it fell with a sharp clatter to the stone floor.

Fearon fought like a tiger, snarling out oaths, and the two men went staggering across the room and eventually fell among the collection of lumber still fighting furiously. Anthony landed underneath, but Fearon's advantage was short-lived, for Darrell and Hallam sprang to the rescue, and dragged him off.

There was a click as the Inspector deftly snapped the handcuffs with which he had provided himself, on the man's wrists, and helpless and beaten, Fearon stood glaring savagely between Hallam and the fat man, an incongruous figure in the black tights and doublet. The handkerchief had been torn off in the struggle, and his face was contorted with passion, and in the dim light of the torch, which still burned upon the packing case, he looked like some demoniacal spirit from another world.

'I think, after all, we shall meet at the Old Bailey,' remarked Anthony quietly, with a grim smile, as he surveyed the captive.

Fearon remained silent, but his eyes flashed his hatred of the man who had been the means of bringing all his plans to naught.

'Bring him downstairs,' said Anthony, as he turned away, and picked up the torch. Grasped firmly on either side by Inspector Hallam and Darrell, and with his hands securely manacled, Fearon was powerless, and apparently this fact was only too apparent to him, for with a supreme effort he mastered his emotion and, shrugging his shoulders, allowed, himself to be led down the stone stairway.

Anthony preceded them, and switched on the lights in the dining room. As he did so, an exclamation behind him caused him to turn quickly.

Pauline, her slim figure wrapped in a pale blue dressing gown, was descending the stairs from the floor above.

'What has happened, Mr. Vyne?' she cried, as she recognised the reporter. 'I heard the noise of a shot somewhere and — '

'It's all right, Miss Langley,' said Anthony hastily. 'You've no cause for alarm. Here, Cunningham,' he called, 'come and tell Miss Langley what has occurred. Take her away into the drawing room or somewhere,' he added in a low tone to the young man, as he hurried forward.

Cunningham complied with alacrity, and led the frightened girl away.

Hallam and Darrell pushed Fearon into the dining room, and he sank down into an armchair.

The man seemed to have completely recovered his sang-froid, for he turned to Anthony with a sneer.

'Well,' he said, 'I suppose you've won. It was a near thing though. You must admit that I ought to have finished you off properly when I had you in that cave. But my love of the dramatic always did get the better of me.' He paused. 'You might offer me a drink, you know.'

Anthony poured some whiskey into a glass, and handed it to Fearon.

The man gulped it down eagerly, and a draught of the spirit brought a touch of colour into his pale face.

'Ah, that's better,' he remarked. 'Well, I'd sooner be hanged than spend any more years in clink, and, anyway, we've all got to die some day.'

The man's callousness was amazing.

No sign of contrition for his many crimes seemed to enter his mind. As he lay back in the chair, the light from the big centre electrolier shone full on his face.

Anthony turned to Hallam with a smile hovering about the corners of his mouth.

'Well, Hallam,' he said quizzically, 'do you recognise him?'

Hallam looked astonished.

'Recognise him!' he repeated in amazement. 'I don't know what you mean.'

'The last time you saw him, he was wearing a beard and moustache,' said Anthony. 'But even without those adornments, it's not difficult. Come, Hallam, think. In a certain flat in Bloomsbury — '
But he got no further.

With a shout, Detective Inspector Hallam leaped to his feet.

'Good God!' he yelled. 'You don't mean — '

'North!' interposed the reporter, 'Derwent North, the murderer of Jonathan Harper!'

The surprise was complete, and Anthony, who loved to stage these little denouements, with the same love that any artist feels for his work when he knows that it is worthy of him, was content.

* * *

It was several hours later. Inspector Person had been 'phoned for, and the whole situation explained to him. He listened in great astonishment, his large mouth wide open, and his eyes almost popping from his head, and after had carted the prisoner off to the local gaol, accompanied by Hallam, where Fearon was to remain temporarily until taken up to London to await his trial.

Anthony, in spite of Darrell's eager questions, had taken advantage of the Inspector's short absence to snatch a few hours much-needed rest, and now, after a bath and a change, he was seated with the others at breakfast.

Hallam had returned from seeing Fearon safely put away in the single cell that the little police station boasted. Sir Owen, feeling much better, had come down to breakfast, and was listening with great interest to Anthony's account of the events of the night.

The morning had started cold and cloudy, but had developed into a fine warm day.

It was very pleasant out on the terrace, for Pauline had caused the meal to be served there, and the little party looked happy and content, and without a care in the world. The cloud which had hung over Langley Towers had been lifted with the capture of Fearon.

Hallam was in great spirits. The arrest of the man meant a lot to him, for he had been dreading his interview with the Chief, and the resultant hauling over the coals which he knew was coming to him for having allowed North, Fearon, as he knew him now, to escape.

'The only thing that remains now,' said Darrell, during one of the very short intervals when his mouth was not full of kidneys and bacon, 'is the hiding place of the treasure.'

'That I shall be pleased to show you all, after breakfast,' said Anthony, leaning back in his chair.

'You've found it, then?' asked Sir Owen in surprise, for he knew nothing of the reporter's experiment of the previous morning.

Anthony shook his head.

'No,' he answered, 'but I've tested your theory, Sir Owen, and feel convinced that it is correct.'

'Then there really is a treasure, after all?' asked Pauline, with a smile.

Sir Owen laughed.

'You've always been rather sceptical about it, haven't you?' he said, 'and, of course, it still remains to be proved, but this will finally settle it one way or the other if Vyne is correct.'

'Well, whether there is any treasure, or not,' put in Hallam, 'Vyne certainly found me the equivalent of one when he captured Geoffrey Fearon.'

Sir Owen frowned suddenly.

'You know the trial will mean a lot of unpleasant publicity,' he said gloomily.

Anthony looked across at him steadily.

'I'm afraid that can't be helped,' he replied. 'After all, like all these things, it will only be a nine days' wonder, and be forgotten.'

'I can't understand yet how you knew that Fearon was North,' said Hallam.

'It was Sir Owen who first gave me the clue,' answered the reporter.

'I?' said the baronet, in surprise.

'Yes, when you mentioned that the letter you had received from Fearon asking for a large sum of money, came from an address in Bloomsbury. At that time, I only guessed, but directly I, saw Fearon, I recognised him in spite of the absence of beard and moustache.'

'I wonder what was the motive for the murder of old Harper?' mused Hallam.

'I think you'll find,' said Anthony, 'that the motive was simply robbery. I think Fearon imagined that Harper kept a lot of jewels in his safe at Bloomsbury, and the old man caught him trying to help himself. He probably threatened to give Fearon away to the police, and Fearon poisoned him by putting cocaine in the water at his bedside, to save himself, afterwards trying to make it look as if Harper had committed suicide. You see, until you searched the old man's flat, you hadn't a scrap of evidence to convict him of being a 'fence', and he knew that; so he could have had Fearon arrested on a charge of attempted robbery with impunity.'

'You're possibly right,' agreed Hallam. 'I can't understand, though, why Harper should have let Fearon live there with him.'

'Fearon had probably in the past had many dealings with the old man,' said Anthony. 'No doubt when Fearon came out of prison, he made straight for Harper. I don't suppose he had any money to go anywhere else, although he hoped to get some from Sir Owen. Harper probably thought he might be useful to him in some of his schemes, and I've no doubt they were quite friendly until Harper found Fearon trying to double-cross him.'

'How did you know that this scoundrel was a relation of mine, Vyne?' asked Sir Owen.

'It is a habit of mine,' said Anthony, 'to make full enquiries into the private lives of everyone connected with any 'story' on which I am working. Directly I learnt from Miss Langley that you had been married before, I made enquiries concerning your first wife. It didn't take me long to discover that she had possessed a brother with a very unsavoury reputation, and who I found out had served several heavy sentences in prison. I asked my paper in London to make further enquiries, the result of which I received this morning.

'Now, previously to this, when Miss Langley came to me with the story of your disappearance, she mentioned that she had seen a figure in black bending over you on the lawn, and afterwards told me, at my request, the legend of the Black Hunchback, and the hidden treasure.

'It seemed clear to me that someone was masquerading as the family ghost, and the only reason I could assign for this was that it would give him a chance of a clear run of the Towers without the risk of anyone making too strict enquiries into his identity should he have ever been seen, as the villagers or anyone who encountered him would rather tend to give him a wide berth from superstitious fear. The reason for wishing to have this free run around the environs of Langley I could not be certain, but I imagined that it might possibly have some connection with the treasure. I then learned that on the night of your disappearance, you had discovered the clue to the bullion's hiding place, and I became certain that the treasure was at the bottom of the whole business.

'The death of Travis, the gamekeeper, never puzzled me very much. The two shots, and the finding of the gold charm, which in no other conceivable way could have got into Travis's hand, except by its being deliberately put there, seeing that, according to Miss Langley, you had only been dressed in pyjamas and dressing gown and would not be likely to be wearing an ornament of that description, enabled me to arrive at the correct solution.

'At that time, of course, I knew nothing about the existence of Fearon, for it was not until I had seen the photograph on the mantelpiece in the drawing room that I knew you had been previously married. Directly I did, and after my enquiries in London, I put two and two together, and when I discovered that he had only recently been released from prison, I became certain that this brother-in-law was the man who was masquerading as the Black Hunchback.

'The attempted abduction of Miss Langley fitted in with my theory that he was trying to force you to disclose the whereabouts of the treasure, and he was trading on your love for your daughter to gain his ends. It was the only theory that would account for the attempts.

'When I discovered you, Sir Owen, in the cave on the hillside, your story confirmed my theory absolutely, although I must confess I never imagined for a moment that Fearon and North were one and the same until I remembered the date that North left his address, and the time the Black Hunchback first appeared here coincided exactly. He knew that he was suspected of the murder of Harper, and what better hiding place could he have found?

'At the same time, he was killing two birds with one stone. He had to have money to enable him to get away, and the treasure presented the only means of gratifying his desires, as you had already refused to help him further.

'I think that practically covers the whole ground, and now as we all appear to have finished breakfast, except, of course, Darrell — but then he generally goes on until lunch time — I will show you where, if Sir Owen's theory respecting the solution of the verse is the true one, the treasure is hidden.'

The others gave an eager assent, and Anthony rose to his feet and led the way down the steps on to the lawn. Crossing this at right angles he presently passed through an opening in the high yew hedge near the rose garden. They found now that they were in an almost direct line with the North Tower.

Anthony proceeded to walk slowly forward in the direction of the Tower. At a little group of trees and bushes he halted, and turned to the others.

'Unless, Sir Owen, I am greatly mistaken,' he said, waving his hand to where, hidden in the bushes, stood a large bronze statue of Hercules, 'the bullion is hidden — there!'

'Where do you mean?' asked the baronet, 'in the statue?'

'Yes,' answered Anthony. 'Look!'

He approached the bushes and gently pulled the ones surrounding the base of the figure aside. The pedestal on which the statue stood, was of marble, and Anthony pointed to a tiny white chipped mark on the grimed stone.

'That is where my rifle bullet struck,' he remarked, 'and the last line of the clue reads: 'Seek there and ye shall find — in chest'.'

He looked up and indicated the massive bronze chest of the figure.

'I think that you will find that the treasure is concealed within that hollow statue,' he said.

'By Jove!' cried Sir Owen, 'I always thought — 'in chest' meant in a chest!'

Anthony nodded.

'I thought that,' he answered, 'but I think it means in the chest of this figure. We can soon prove whether we are right, or not.'

'There must be some way of opening this statue without destroying it, otherwise the treasure could never have been hidden there,' he continued. 'According to the legend, old Sir Ralph hadn't got much time in which to conceal the bullion.'

While he had been talking, he had hoisted himself up on to the top of the base, and now began to make a close inspection of the weather-beaten bronze.

It was difficult to find any trace of the method by which the bullion had been introduced into the figure, if indeed it had ever been put there at all, for time and exposure had filled up any faint crack or mark that might have formed a clue to the secret.

The others watched breathlessly, as Anthony made his close examination, and even the usually phlegmatic Hallam showed traces of excitement.

Suddenly the reporter gave a little exclamation and his eyes gleamed.

'I believe I've got it,' he said.

He was standing on tip-toe, and peering at the massive neck of the figure.

'I can't get close enough to see properly,' he continued, 'but there appears to me to be a faint line just where the head fits on to the neck.'

'Let me look,' cried Cunningham. 'I

can get up closer than you can.'

He dragged himself up on to the marble base, and from thence swung himself up until he was kneeling on one of the massive arms of the statue.

'You're quite right,' he cried, a second later. 'There's a line that goes right round the neck just below the chin.'

'That's it,' said Anthony. 'I think you'll find that the entire head unscrews!'

'Let's try and see,' cried the girl, her eyes shining with excitement.

'That's easier said than done,' replied Anthony. 'Don't forget that this hasn't been touched for centuries and has now, owing to the action of the elements, practically become part of the body of the statue. It's going to take time and a considerable amount of strength to loosen it.'

Cunningham had produced a penknife, and was scraping round the faint line energetically.

'Wait a moment,' said Sir Owen, 'I'll get some oil.'

He hurried off towards the house, and a few minutes later returned with an oil can.

Frank had scraped off the dirt that had accumulated, and now the crack was plainly visible.

Anthony took the oil-can from the baronet and handed it up to the young man.

Cunningham grasped it, and proceeded to squirt all the way round the crack in the statue's neck. The joint fitted close, but he hoped some of the oil would find its way in.

He dropped the oil-can and grasping the huge head with both hands exerted all his strength and turned. It refused to budge the fraction of an inch!

'Try it the other way,' suggested Hallam.

Cunningham did so, but without result.

'You'll require more than one person on that,' said Anthony. 'Where can we find a ladder?'

'I'll get one,' said Sir Owen, and set off at a run towards a shed at the foot of the Tower.

While he was gone Frank continued to tug at the head until he was red in the face with his exertions. Sir Owen returned presently with a short ladder, and Anthony took it, wedging it firmly against the statue. Then the reporter mounted, and together he and Cunningham grasped the head.

The veins stood out like cords on Anthony's forehead, as he put forward every ounce of his enormous strength. There came a sharp creak, and he felt the head give slightly to the left.

'Come on,' he panted, 'again!'

This time it swung completely round! Six turns they gave it, and it was free of the trunk. It took both of them all their strength to lift it away, but they succeeded and dropped it on the soft mould by the bushes.

Anthony peered into the interior of the statue thus revealed. Piled high, almost to the top, were dozens and dozens of bars of some tarnished metal.

Anthony opened his knife and, taking out one of the bars, gently scraped it. It was pure gold!

17

The Last of Geoffrey Fearon

Nearly eight months had passed. Busy months for Anthony, and the trial of Geoffrey Fearon had occupied but a small portion of his time.

It had, however, created quite a sensation, and while it lasted had been the sole topic of conversation in the newspapers, *The Messenger* of course, securing the scoop of its life.

The verdict had been a foregone conclusion from the outset, and although Fearon's counsel strove valiantly on his behalf, in the face of overwhelming evidence brought forward by Hallam, it was impossible for him to do any good. Without leaving the box the jury returned a verdict of guilty.

Shortly after the sentence Geoffrey Fearon had made a full confession which included an account of the murder of old Jonathan Harper, and almost word for word it tallied with Anthony's theory as to what had taken place.

It was the morning fixed for the execution, and as Anthony sat in his flat waiting for Darrell, who had telephoned to say he was coming along, he idly scanned the morning's papers. His thoughts wandered back to the man who had so nearly been the means of ending his career, and his eyes strayed to the clock. In little more than a quarter of an hour, Fearon would have expiated his many crimes and gone beyond reach of earthly judgment.

It was a solemn thought, and Anthony lay back in his chair, his papers unheeded, his eyes fixed unseeingly upon the white ceiling.

What strange kink was it that sent a human being upon the path of crime? Some slight alteration in the fine delicate cells of the brain, and he, too, might have been a criminal, thought Anthony. It was like a piece of grit in some high-powered engine; a speck of dust in the lens of. a microscope; a foreign body that ruined and destroyed the whole delicate mechanism, a touch of insanity that turned an otherwise sane man into a covetous being for ever at war against society, and always living with the knowledge that sooner or later Nemesis in the form of the law must overtake and destroy him. Anthony roused himself from his reverie.

The clock pointed to one minute to eight. Sixty seconds more, and the soul of Geoffrey Fearon would have left this world to roam no one knew whither.

The clock commenced to strike the hour of eight, and almost unconsciously Anthony rose to his feet and stood until it had finished chiming.

And so Darrell found him, as the stout man came quietly into the room.

Frost brought up the morning mail, and beside the usual pile of letters, there was a large registered package.

The reporter picked it up, and noted that the post-mark was Buckinghamshire.

'I wonder who this is from,' he remarked as he cut the string.

Inside was a wooden box, and removing the lid Anthony found wrapped carefully in cotton wool a little golden figure. It stood some eight inches high, and was a model of the Hercules statue in the grounds of Langley Towers, finely wrought in purest gold.

'Ah!' said Anthony, 'a present from Sir Owen. A little memento. In all probability made from some of the original bullion.'

'It's rather beautiful, isn't it?' said Darrell admiringly.

'Very,' agreed Anthony, and added: 'But what a coincidence that it should have arrived this morning of all mornings.'

The stout man looked surprised for a moment. Then he remembered and understood.

At that moment, Frost arrived with breakfast, and under the cheering atmosphere of the meal, the reporter's spirits revived somewhat until they became almost normal, but every now and then his eyes would stray to the little golden statuette of Hercules, which he had placed upon the mantelpiece, and Darrell, happening to catch his friend's gaze on one of these occasions, saw that Anthony Vyne's expression was a very thoughtful one.

Books by Gerald Verner
in the Linford Mystery Library:

THE LAST WARNING
DENE OF THE SECRET SERVICE
THE NURSERY RHYME MURDERS
TERROR TOWER
THE CLEVERNESS OF MR. BUDD
THE SEVEN LAMPS
THEY WALK IN DARKNESS
THE HEEL OF ACHILLES
DEAD SECRET
MR. BUDD STEPS IN
THE RETURN OF MR. BUDD
MR. BUDD AGAIN
QUEER FACE
THE CRIMSON RAMBLERS
GHOST HOUSE
THE ANGEL
DEATH SET IN DIAMONDS
THE CLUE OF THE GREEN CANDLE
THE 'Q' SQUAD
MR. BUDD INVESTIGATES
THE RIVER HOUSE MYSTERY
NOOSE FOR A LADY
THE FACELESS ONES
GRIM DEATH

MURDER IN MANUSCRIPT
THE GLASS ARROW
THE THIRD KEY
THE ROYAL FLUSH MURDERS
THE SQUEALER
MR. WHIPPLE EXPLAINS
THE SEVEN CLUES
THE CHAINED MAN
THE HOUSE OF THE GOAT
THE FOOTBALL POOL MURDERS
THE HAND OF FEAR
SORCERER'S HOUSE
THE HANGMAN
THE CON MAN
MISTER BIG
THE JOCKEY
THE SILVER HORSESHOE
THE TUDOR GARDEN MYSTERY
THE SHOW MUST GO ON
SINISTER HOUSE
THE WITCHES' MOON
ALIAS THE GHOST
THE LADY OF DOOM

with Chris Verner:
THE BIG FELLOW